Foreword

In early December last year, I saw a news report of a large bushfire burning in Queensland, Australia and thought, that's unusually early for bushfire season. I shrugged and got on with life. You see, I live in Perth, Western Australia, some 5000 kilometres or more away from that fire burning near the East Coast. I noted that some blamed global warming, and some blamed the proponents of global warming in forcing the governments to cut back on burning off programs in winter to reduce the amount of carbon being put in the atmosphere. Again, I shrugged and got on with life.

Since then the number and intensity of the fires have spread exponentially, and as I write this, every single state in Australia is suffering major fires, many hopelessly out of control. Estimates of how many and how big vary, but one source says as of today 17.9 million acres of Australia have burned in one of the country's worst fire seasons on record. That's an area larger than West Virginia, and more than eight times the area that burned in California in 2018—and the fires are still burning out of control.

I find, when people talk really big numbers I switch off, because they are too big to contemplate, however, another report says that well over one billion native animals and birds have lost their lives…one billion.

Like most Australians I wanted to do something about it. But what could I do other than give money, which I have done. The problem is that it's nowhere near enough; a tiny drop in the ocean of what is needed. Then I had an idea.

I am very fortunate as a writer to have a wonderful publisher in the US, The Wild Rose Press, and a part of the benefit is that I belong to an author group under the auspices of TWRP. We have a forum loop, where we assist each other in all sorts of areas; it is a wonderful feeling of comradeship as everyone experiences the same issues, frustrations, and joys. I sent an email to the loop asking if there was any interest in authors donating a short story and foregoing any royalties so that all proceeds could be donated to the bushfire appeal if there was enough for an anthology. I thought if I could generate some interest, hopefully I could ask TWRP to publish it, but that if it did not seem feasible from a logistical point of view, I would seek help and self-publish it, because as an author, what better way is there for me to help those who have lost everything, than to write?

Well, the response was phenomenal and over the weekend that followed I received over four hundred emails pledging stories, support, editorial help and a narrator to perform an audio version. Best of all, the President of TWRP, Rhonda Penders, emailed me, even though she was away, expressing her enthusiasm and willingness to support such an anthology.

I started out by hoping I could coax a dozen or so authors to give me a story they would lose the rights to, yet by Sunday night I had forty-four of them! And all of those who didn't or couldn't have a story ready for the deadline, without exception, wanted to help in whatever way they could. Most (but not all) live in the US and news had travelled to them just how bad the fires are, and everyone's generosity was wonderful. In fact, I had so many offers to help edit, format, cover design, narrate, even a self-publishing route was doable. Then Rhonda emailed again just before I was to crash into bed exhausted, to say she had spoken with her partner, RJ, and they wanted to take over the publishing. My dream suddenly became reality and this book you are reading took wings.

I have so many people to thank, I can't even begin to for fear I will miss some, but you all know who you are and I, and all the people of Australia thank you for your generosity of time and spirit to make this happen.

Also, thank you dear reader for buying this anthology, and supporting the victims of the worst fire ever. I sincerely hope you enjoy some of the best authors I know as they each present a tale they chose to donate. Some of these stories took a long time to write, edit, re-write, and edit a whole lot more, yet each was willing to give it to you.

Please enjoy, and sincerely, thank you.

Stephen B King
Perth, Western Australia
13th January 2020

Australia Burns

Volume 2
A collection of Romance, Young Adult, and Women's Fiction Short Stories

All proceeds from this publication will be donated to one or more organizations assisting in the fire relief effort in Australia.

Australia Burns, Volume Two

The Wild Rose Press, Inc.
PO Box 708
Adams Basin, NY 14410-0708
Visit us at www.thewildrosepress.com

Publishing History
First Edition, 2020
Print ISBN 978-1-5092-3104-1
Digital ISBN 978-1-5092-3105-8

Published in the United States of America

Table of Contents

Che Gelida Manina
by

M. S. Spencer

"I don't want to stay here, Amelia."

"But Mother, you love Sarasota! You love the sun, the people, the beach. Why this sudden desire to move to Morocco?"

"It's always been a dream of mine." Grace knew her daughter wouldn't buy it but didn't want to tell her how desperately she needed to get away from Florida. Since Jack died nine months before on Christmas Eve, she couldn't bear to go to the Gulf…or listen to his favorite opera, *La Bohème*…or even light candles at dinner. Jack had been the most romantic man in the world and the love of her life. Now that he was gone, all desire for romance had gone with him. It was only because of her promise to him to stay through one last Christmas that she had remained. *I'll keep my promise, but I'll be out of here by Boxing Day.*

"Well, it makes no sense." Amelia switched gears. "Just yesterday Brad was saying you should come up here to Portland—"

"Not on your life. I may be a doting grandmother, but I don't think I could handle twin toddlers twenty-four-seven."

The woman at the other end of the phone sniffed. "*Hmmph.* Well, we don't want you alone on Christmas Eve, Mother. Brad would be happy to book a flight for you."

"You know I can't, dear."

"Oh, bother the promise. Dad would understand."

Grace thought of Jack's last whispered request. "No, he wouldn't."

"Okay, okay." Amelia paused. "Did you sign up for Friends.com yet?"

"No, and stop badgering me."

"All I ask is that you think about it. It's about time you got out of the house. The site's supposed to have a 90 percent success rate in matching people."

"I doubt that. Gotta go, dear." Grace hung up and stared at the website on her computer screen. She hesitated, then clicked "Your Friends.com Profile." She wrote quickly and furiously, tossing her thoughts out before she lost her nerve.

Recently widowed woman, 60, seeking companion for excursions—bird-watching and sightseeing. Not interested in romance or personal confidences. No moonlit beach walkers please. No candlelight dinners. Love of opera a deal-breaker.

She typed in her credit card number and clicked "Submit," then returned to her profile and reread it. "Oh dear, that sounds awfully negative…"

Her finger hovered over the "Delete Post" button when a message popped up. "Edward Harper has emailed you." She opened it.

Widower, 62, happy to oblige. Coffee today?

Next to the message was a man's photograph. She studied it, trying to plumb its secrets—a broad face, the planes of the cheeks flat and tanned. Little crinkles of skin at each temple hinted at a quiet sense of humor. His bright hazel eyes under a thatch of brown hair smiled at her, as if willing her to say hello. She pressed "Reply" and typed in, "Yes."

An hour later, she sat in a booth in the Gray Dolphin Café, wondering if she'd recognize him. A tall man came through the automatic doors and strode resolutely toward her. "Are you Grace?"

I can deny it. I can get up and walk out right now. The eyes held her. Cheerful, calm, intelligent. "Yes. Won't you join me?"

He slid onto the seat and ordered coffee for the two of them. Grace, having had to deal with the world on her own for the last few months, found it refreshing. He had a way of making her feel comfortable and pampered at the same time. Two hours later, they parted at the café door.

She didn't hear from him that day, or the next, or the next. Exactly one week later, an email popped up. "Coffee today?"

Fingers scampering quickly over the keys, she typed, "Yes."

They met at the café, but Edward drew her outside. "How about a walk through Robinson Preserve? I brought binoculars. And coffee."

"Sure."

Two hours later, he left her at the café entrance. She almost asked if he'd like to see her again, but didn't.

Precisely a week later, he called. "Coffee?"

This time she was ready. "Would you care to go to Spanish Point with me? It's a historic site."

"Certainly—I was going to suggest something similar. I'll pick you up at the café."

And so it went for two months. The two of them met every Wednesday and toured local sights like Marie Selby Gardens, Ringling's Cà d'Zan, and Ybor City. Edward proved a perfect escort—knowledgeable, funny, interested in everything. Grace's life came to revolve around the weekly dates. She'd find herself thinking about him every day, wondering more and more often how he felt about her. After all, he never asked her personal questions. If she inquired about his past, he would demur. "We are but fellow travelers. That was the deal, wasn't it?"

Whenever his reticence grated on her, she would reread her Friends.com profile. *You asked for this, Grace. In fact, you insisted upon it.* Then she would pour herself a drink and watch another re-run of *Love Boat*.

As the weeks passed, Grace sank deeper and deeper into a funk. Edward was careful to keep his distance—the occasional touch on the hand or squeeze of the elbow meant only that he wanted to draw her attention to something. She began to covet the delicate brush of his fingers across her skin. Sometimes she would even bump into him, pretending to be absorbed in a painting or view.

She had said goodbye to him one Wednesday, facing the emptiness of the week ahead. Sitting in her car, it suddenly struck her as unfair. *Is this all he can give? One afternoon a week for the rest of my life?* She checked her face in the rearview mirror. Wrinkles spiraled through the once blooming cheeks. Her hair had begun the gradual but depressing transformation to pure white, and her once cobalt blue eyes had faded to the cerulean of a misty morning sky. She started the engine. "I've got to ask him."

But as the days dragged by, she did nothing. Time and again she would click on Edward's address, only to hesitate. *I'm not ready.*

That Sunday Amelia called. "I hope you'll reconsider and come for Christmas, Mother."

Christmas. Christ. In her preoccupation with Edward, she had lost track of the date. In three weeks her vow to Jack would be discharged. *What difference would it make if I left a few days early?* Unexpectedly, Edward's smiling face flashed before her. Yearning vied with terror, threatening to rip her heart apart. *I'm not ready. I need to get out of here.* She finally managed, "Perhaps I will."

"Wonderful! Come a week early—that way we'll have plenty of time to catch up."

"All right."

As her departure approached, Grace put off informing Edward. *I know him. He'll nod silently. He won't even ask if I need a ride to the airport.* She stifled the stab of pain.

The day before she was to leave, she finally confessed. His eyes, for once, did not smile, but he was silent. She waved him off at the café and went home to finish packing. As she locked the suitcase, cold reality sluiced like ice water down her back. *I guess this is it.* She looked around the cozy bungalow Edward had never entered. And yet he seemed so much a part of it, of her life now. The longing she'd felt for him—longing that she refused to acknowledge—exploded into desire. *I want him. I want to hold him. And I want to talk—really talk—pour out all my thoughts and my childhood dreams, my needs, my fears.*

To silence the pleas, she did something she hadn't done since Jack died—she took the shell path to the water. The beach was empty, and she walked until her feet hurt—a mile, two miles, three. As she walked, the sun began to descend in one of those glorious Florida sunsets that make you wonder if you've landed on another planet. The white powdery sand crunched between her toes. *How I've missed this! Maybe I was wrong to cut myself off from the things I loved.*

By the time she arrived back at the shell path, it was nearly dark. She turned for one last look at the moon and stars. A beach chair sat forlornly on the shore, waves lapping at its legs. Something fluttered from it. *Oh, right, I left my towel there.*

As she approached, a silvery tenor began to croon Jack's favorite aria from *La Bohème*. In it, Rodolfo sings to his new love Mimi, "*Che gelida manina*—What a cold little hand you have!"

She rounded on the chair. "Edward?"

He sat up. "Grace?"

She wanted to run into his arms. She wanted to kiss his lips, his forehead, his hands. Instead, she stood quietly, her arms at her sides. "Edward, what are you doing here? I thought you hated the beach."

His eyes bored into her. "Not me. You. You didn't want romance. You didn't want to hold my hand, or light a candle, or hear my music. I respected your wishes."

She ached to cry out, "I was wrong! Edward, I want to be with you!" But fear clogged her throat. *I'm not ready.* All she could manage was, "Yes."

His lips twisted. "Yes." Then he stood up and walked away across the sand. Grace watched helplessly as the second love of her life left her.

She went to bed, but the hours ticked by as she lay awake, by turns angry and despondent. The next morning she called Amelia. "I've decided to stay here through Christmas Eve."

"Mother? Why? You'll be so lonely!"

"No! No, I'll be fine. I have a promise to keep. I'll fly up Christmas day."

She checked the calendar. Four days to go to Christmas Eve. She had to find Edward before she left. *I can't leave without telling him about Jack—without explaining my earlier aversion to romance.* She turned on the laptop and typed his name in the search box.

The first list turned up three dozen Edward Harpers, ten of whom lived in the Sarasota area. She spent two days tracking them down, leaving messages at the most promising leads. Then she sat down to wait.

Christmas Eve arrived without any word from Edward. Her suitcase stood ready by the door. As the light faded, she went outside to her patio. *La Bohème* played softly from inside. *I can't lose him. Why didn't I tell him? What was I afraid of?* The pain? *You fool, the pain found you anyway.* At least she had the beach and the music back. Only one more thing to do. She rose, found some matches, and lit the Christmas candle. As she watched the flame flicker in the evening breeze, she savored an uneasy peace. *Perhaps it's for the best. I'll leave tomorrow and forget all about him.*

Someone moved from the darkness into the light. She sprang up to find bright hazel eyes smiling into hers. He touched her hand and sang softly, "*Che gelida manina*. What a cold little hand you have, my dear. May I warm it?"

She gave it to him, then led him down the path to the beach.

Recipes for Love
by

Carol Henry

Brooke desperately scanned her grandmother's old, dog-eared cookbook. Conner was coming for dinner tonight, and she'd do anything—anything at all—to rekindle that old spark, even if it meant force-feeding him love potions. He would never know what hit him once he opened his mouth and savored every bite.

The cookbook, cover missing with tattered pages, was strewn with carefully penciled-in notes. She smiled, picturing Grandma Gussy sitting at the kitchen table, her nose to her notes, as she clutched her pencil close to the tip, almost writing with her fingernail. Brooke fanned through the pages and spotted a folded sheet opened to *Seafood Fantasies*. She ran her fingers down the page until they landed on *Oysters*.

"Oysters stimulate arousal."

Yes! She wasn't sure she would like oysters, but Conner ate anything that was put in front of him. He always cleaned up his plate. Fortunately for him, he had no problem with his weight, as he worked out three times a week, ran five miles a day, and played ball at the men's sports club on weekends. She'd order a dozen oysters on the half shell from a local restaurant and follow her grandmother's suggestions for serving them.

She added oysters to her shopping list.

She turned to another marked page. Bingo! *Love Salad!* Arugula, almonds, and avocado sprinkled with sweet basil and cilantro seed to induce sensuous passion.

Oh my God! All in one dish! What luck! Who needed an entrée? Although a salad would go great with the vegetarian lasagna she planned to serve. Conner would be so stuffed with burning love once he finished his salad he wouldn't know what hit him. But just in case, she flipped to desserts. *Yes! Yes! Yes!* How to stimulate the male libido. *Pine Nut Cookies! Oh my*. She wasn't into baking cookies, but these sounded easy-peasy. And it would be a light dessert after eating the lasagna. She'd make sure they weren't overbaked so they would be soft and moist.

"Add a teaspoon of freshly grated ginger to spice things up."

What a minute. What were pine nuts? She'd never heard of them. Did they come from pine trees? Surely not from pine cones! Whatever, she'd comb the grocery store aisles until she found them and make those cookies. Why not? She might just add two teaspoons of ginger and a dash of nutmeg just for good measure. If the oysters and salad didn't work, these cookies were sure to do the trick.

She wrote pine nuts, ginger, and nutmeg on her shopping list and underlined them as imperative that she find them. The list was growing. Hopefully the local market would have all the ingredients.

She wasn't big on wines, but she'd go to the local wine store and ask their advice for a pairing in her price range to go with her meal. Although, if it took a few extra dollars to help sway his feelings, she'd hand over a few extra bucks for a bottle. Perhaps a bottle of sparkling strawberry moscato. She knew Conner was more of a beer guy, but perhaps for once he'd indulge her and sip some, just to humor her. Weren't strawberries one of those fruits that induced something enticing? He could always have a beer later—after he'd fallen madly in love with her once again.

One could only hope.

Scanning the cookbook once again, she searched for a section on strawberries just to make sure. *Bingo!* An excellent source of potassium, which helped regulate the electrolytes that lowered chances of heart attack and stroke. After the night she had planned with Conner, he would need all the potassium his body could handle.

She grabbed her grocery list, her purse, and car keys, then donned her jacket, slipping her hands in the sleeves as she went out the door. She didn't have a minute to waste, and she had to pick up her sister Saundra, who had taken her car in to the local garage to have the tires rotated. She pulled in as Saundra was getting out of her vehicle.

"I'll just be a minute." Her sister waved as she ran across the parking lot. "Got to give them my keys. Be right out." The door slammed behind her.

Brooke sat in the car, her hands drumming on the steering wheel. She and Conner had had many good times over the years. It was hard to say just what had gone wrong. He'd started slipping further and further away from her over the past six months. Sure, they had had their disagreements, but it wasn't anything they hadn't talked through and moved on. In fact, they had always gotten along so well their friends were jealous of their relationship.

So what went wrong? She had tried to talk to him, but every time she mentioned anything about his listlessness, he shut down. If this meal didn't do the trick, it wouldn't be for lack of her trying to add a spark to their romance. If nothing else, it might loosen his tongue and she'd find out just what was going on. She hoped and prayed it wasn't another woman.

Saundra opened the passenger door and slid into the seat, sliding the seatbelt across her chest. "So. What's up? Why the sad look? I thought you were excited Conner was coming for dinner tonight. Isn't that why you're going shopping?"

"Yes. And I am excited. In fact, I've been thumbing through Grandma Gussy's old recipe book and found some wonderful recipes that might just get Conner in the swing of things tonight. I've got my list."

"Oh Lordy, you really don't think those recipes are going to get Conner in the mood, do you? They're all old wives' tales."

"I don't know. The explanation behind some of those ingredients sound real enough to me. It's worth a try, don't you think?"

"Sure. But don't be disappointed if nothing works. What's with that guy, anyway?"

"I'm hoping to find out tonight. Maybe just eating a delicious dinner will be satisfying enough to put him in the mood to open up and tell me what's going on."

"Sounds to me as if nothing is 'going on.' Maybe you should dump him and find someone else."

"Really? You think it's that easy? How can I just turn off this burning love for Conner after all these years?"

"Well, it's been a long time for sure. Perhaps it's time to turn him loose."

"So you and Austen never had any problems before you got married. Not only high school sweethearts, but childhood sweethearts. I'm not so lucky, I guess."

"Okay, so I'll go shopping with you and help you find all these wonderful aphrodisiac foods."

"You don't have to go with me. I can handle this on my own."

"We are still sitting in the parking lot, and time is running out. Let me go with you—I can help so you'll be home in plenty of time to start cooking. When is Conner coming over?"

"Seven. He has a board meeting that starts at five."

"Plenty of time. Give me your list and let's get going."

****

Later that afternoon the house steamed with warm, enticing smells. Candles flickered low on the table set for two. She'd dug out her grandmother's rosewood china, crystal goblets, and silverware. She'd even washed and pressed one of her antique white damask tablecloths she'd picked up at an auction. A fresh pineapple sat in the center of the table as decoration, with whole lemons and limes surrounding the bottom. At the last minute she placed several plump strawberries in between the yellow and green fruit. She and Saundra had found them in the fresh produce section and couldn't resist. She'd left nothing to chance. If nothing else, just looking at the display, smelling the pineapple and citrus, and thinking about the sweet, juicy, homeopathic properties of the pineapple would stir the senses. Well, maybe not, but it was a great centerpiece.

The lasagna was out of the oven, the oysters would be ready any minute, and the salad was cooling in the refrigerator, as was the wine.

The doorbell rang. Brooke ran to it in anticipation. When she opened it, her heart skipped a beat. Conner looked so sexy in his sporty tan slacks and golf shirt; his biceps and flat abs were hard to miss. His smile was dynamite. She threw her arms around his neck, anticipating a kiss. He gave her a quick peck on the cheek and moved past her into the main hall.

Her heart sank. The evening wasn't starting out very well. She pasted a smile on her face, sighed, and followed him down the hall.

"You're just in time. I thought we'd start with oysters on the half shell."

"Sorry, I don't like oysters."

She stopped in her tracks, her hands on her hips. "What do you mean you don't like oysters? All men like oysters. I made them especially for you."

They'd gone to three different stores looking for them.

"Sorry. I wish you would have asked sooner. I thought you were making lasagna."

"I did. But I thought these would make a great appetizer. Never mind. We can start with the salad. You like salad, don't you?"

"Yes."

She breathed a sigh of relief. Her salad teemed with stimulants.

"How about a glass of wine?"

"Great. After the meeting I just had, I could use a glass of something. Not sure wine is going to do the trick, but I'll give it a try."

"Have a seat in the dining room. There is a bottle in the wine tub. You can pour us each a glass while I get the salad."

Brooke carried the bowl of salad, along with the wooden tongs, to the table and handed it to him in anticipation of him taking a hearty portion. The salad alone should have him opening up and coming around the table professing his love.

"What's this?" Conner asked as he placed the bowl in front of him and dished himself a large portion.

"My grandmother's special salad recipe."

He looked into the salad plate in front of him and frowned.

"Are these almonds? I'm allergic to nuts."

Why didn't she know that? They'd been together long enough she should have known that. Like the oysters—the whole night was turning into a disaster. Not sure what his allergic reaction to nuts was all about, but she was beginning to think she wanted to find out.

"As a matter of fact, they are almonds."

She watched him pick the nuts out of the salad. Her romantic desires plummeted. *Nuts!*

"This isn't lettuce, and what are these slimy green chunks…?"

"You know, maybe we should just skip the salad," she said. "Let's sip some wine?" The urge to grab a hammer was strong; a jolt to the noggin might jog his sex drive, or open his tongue to finally tell her what was wrong with their relationship. Feeding him those pine nut cookies was beginning to sound like a great idea. But she loved him too much to kill him with a cookie.

She served the store-bought vegetable lasagna. He dug in with gusto. She caught him glancing at the centerpiece several times and groaned. Oh, why had she bothered?

"That was great." He grinned with satisfaction. "All those carrots, parsnips, mushrooms, and tomatoes hit the spot."

Her head shot up. Her grandmother's book had mentioned these vegetables. Maybe all was not lost.

He smiled at her. She definitely couldn't serve him those cookies now.

"I'm sorry about dessert. The cookies have nuts."

He reached across the table, took her hand in his, and looked into her eyes.

Was it the carrots? The parsnips?

"Don't worry," he whispered, leaning closer, his warm breath stirring the tendrils around her ears. "I was wondering…"

He rubbed the sensitive spot in her palm with his thumb, slow, sensual, erotic swirls. *Ohhh yes.* The sparks were still there.

"Yes," she whispered. "Yes, Conner?"

"Well…do you think we could do something about that pineapple? It's been driving me crazy. Maybe squeeze the juice out, add some rum, get cozy out under the stars…"

The pineapple! My centerpiece is driving him crazy?

She grabbed the pineapple and danced all the way to the kitchen. Finally, something that stirred his arousal. All was not lost. If he wanted pineapple and rum out under the stars, he'd get pineapple and rum out under the stars. And lots of it.

Waiting for Caleb
by

Gini Rifkin

Kansas 1852

Caleb had been gone for over two years, but the dreaded letter had arrived only three months ago. He'd called the note his *just in case* letter and promised to keep it with him at all times while in the goldfields of California. Why was it, with this proof of his demise, she couldn't truly believe her husband was dead? Something inside her heart and soul told her to keep waiting—to keep hoping.

He'd gone off with his friend, Yancy, saying he wanted to provide a better life for Emmy. She knew he also left because he'd been born with a bit of wanderlust. She liked that about Caleb, his love for adventure, and life in general.

But wanderlust or not, it had been Yancy's urging that had turned the trick. While she was glad Caleb hadn't gone off alone, she didn't always cotton to Yancy's ideas—or feel he was the best influence for her husband. Sometimes Yancy would stand too close to her, and she caught him staring a time or two in a less than *good friend* sort of way. But what was done was done. Now they were both gone.

The hardest times were the winters. Long dark lonely nights—and nonstop cold. By the end of the day she was glad to fall exhausted into bed, at least there she was warm for a while beneath the quilts and blankets.

This morning, from the window, she'd seen and heard the wild geese flying high and honking with joy.

Such a beautiful sight in their lopsided V. But also a sign a storm was in the offing. She shouldn't complain. The winter wheat, planted for her by her kindly neighbor, could use the moisture. Hopefully, whatever was coming wouldn't be a brutal blizzard. Last year's harvest had partially been ruined by a spring hail storm. She needed this crop to grow and thrive if she was going to make it on her own another year out here.

The winter was hard, mentally and physically, on both man and beast—not to mention on a woman.

She shrugged into Caleb's old coat. The too long sleeves hung down passed her hands, a blessing as her mittens had holes and needed mending. Warm hands were also welcomed by Geraldine, her milk goat.

Grabbing a handful of hay, Emmy enticed her obstinate barn buddy over to the milking stand. Getting Geraldine situated was a battle, but once the milking started and Emmy regaled Geraldine with a story or two, the goat settled down and contentedly chewed her cud.

Today, she would tell the goat of the dream she'd had last night about Caleb. She didn't often dream about her husband—which made her both sad and glad. She missed him terribly, of course, and being with him in the dream-world seemed so wonderful, so real. But when she woke up, it meant saying good bye to him all over again. And that hurt deeply. Although this time, it seemed different, more of a visitation then a crazy disjointed escapade. Caleb said they would be together soon. What did that mean? Having received his special letter, she had to face the fact he might be dead. Was she soon to die as well?

She shivered at the unwelcome thought, then covered and set the pail of milk aside. After rewarding

Geraldine with a carefully rationed-out bit of grain, she turned the goat loose to nibble on the brown stubble of grass still available along the south side of the barn.

Her muscles, stiff from bending forward and balancing on the milking stool, she stretched her back and rotated her shoulders as she crossed the barn to feed Ruby. Dear Ruby. The big mule was a Godsend. Not only for helping around the farm, but for transportation to the far-flung neighbors, or pulling the cart to town for supplies. Emmy loved Ruby.

Head hanging over the stall door, the mule watched with bright hopeful eyes, huffing and murmuring in anticipation of breakfast. After planting a kiss on her soft muzzle, Emmy tossed an armful of grass hay over the barrier. Ruby nodded her approval, and with a few mincing sidesteps, she went to work on her allotment.

Opening the indoor pen, Emmy shooed Mama Goose and the ducks from the barn to their outside enclosure. Seeing them waddle along always gave her a smile. Some said they had small brains, but they seemed to understand her and follow direction better than some critters—Geraldine for instance. But truth be told, she loved the goat too. When the fowl were enclosed and protected from land and overhead predators, Emmy returned to the barn.

With her thoughts far away, she filled water buckets and mucked out stalls. Daydreaming happy thoughts, she recalled the time Caleb had returned from hunting with not only a years' worth of venison dinners, but a bouquet of wild flowers he'd bothered to pick in the middle of such an exhausting daytrip. And then there was the cupboard he'd built for her in which to keep her dishes safe and dust free. He'd hammered the present together in the barn, covering it every night with an old threadbare sheet so she couldn't see what he built until he brought it into the cabin on Christmas Day. That was the year before he left. Such good times. She couldn't believe he was gone forever.

Morning chores done, she set aside the shovel and broom and glanced up as the cat leaped out of the rafters. Laughing, she caught Jumpin' Juniper in midair. Sleeping safe and warm up high, the barn cat surveyed her domain, watched for mice, and supervised all that went on down below. With a propensity for surprise flying ambushes, it had been easy to come up with the name for their good and faithful pussycat.

Setting Juniper on the ground, Emmy headed for the house. The wind was up now and blowing straight out of the north.

****

The snow commenced in earnest. And it continued to fall all afternoon and into the night. Emmy ignored the weather as best as she could. She baked bread and hauled in wood, and after slipping and sliding to the barn for evening chores, she could barely keep her eyes open long enough to eat a bite of stew.

Covers tucked almost up to her neck, she reread all of Caleb's letter, even the last one. Still she couldn't believe he was really gone? Blowing out the candle, she prayed wherever he was, here or in the great beyond, he was safe.

About to doze off, she heard a terrible sound. Geraldine was bleating as only a terribly agitated goat could do. What could possibly be wrong? Any bears would be hibernating, and with the storm howling almost as loud as the goat, there was little chance a polecat or fox would be out hunting and causing trouble.

Silently pleading for the goat to stop, Emmy closed her eyes and burrowed deeper into the downy bed. From the first day they'd gotten her home, Geraldine had elected herself to be the watchdog of the barn. If all was not well, with everyone in their assigned place for the night, she felt obligated to send out an earsplitting nagging alarm. Maybe the wind had set her off.

Emmy tried to wait her out. But the noise didn't stop, if fact it got worse. Now Ruby added her guttural brays to the mix.

Something truly had to be wrong.

Leaping from the bed, Emmy pulled on as many clothes as she could find. Boots on, rifle in one hand, and bundled up to the point of hardly being able to walk, she struggled against the wind to the barn.

Rather than standing in her nice warm stall, Ruby was out in the attached run. That couldn't be good. "What's wrong old girl?" She petted and crooned to the mule, but couldn't get her to calm down. Now Ruby produced a muttering sound, one she liked to make just for Caleb. Emmy's dream from the night before came rushing back in full force, and she glanced around half expecting to see her husband standing nearby.

The mule grew increasingly agitated. She charged about, nearly knocking Emmy aside. She kicked at the fence, right where it was weakest and in need of repair. The boards gave way, and Ruby was gone in an instant.

"No Ruby no. Don't run."

Slogging through the foot-high snow, Emmy followed the tracks left by the mule gone wild. Soon she gasped for breath, her energy waning. Tears threatened but froze oh her lashes before they could fall. "Ruby,

Ruby. Please come back." She began to think they would both perish in the storm.

Up ahead, Ruby skidded to a stop, and head down she nosed something lying in the snow up against a rocky ridge. It looked like a person. Stumbling and floundering forward Emmy dropped to her knees.

Caleb? Tired and cold she feared she was dreaming again, only this time with eyes wide open. No, it was really him. She touched his face and smoothed his hair back from his brow.

"Caleb, Caleb, wake up." Now tears of joy threatened.

He moaned and rolled his head from side to side. She felt along his body trying to determine if he were injured—he didn't cry out when she moved his arms and legs. That was a good sign. They had to get back to the cabin. She shook him awake. He worked at focusing his gaze upon her face, and then he smiled. "Emmy. I knew you'd be waiting for me."

Emmy roused Caleb to his feet, but getting him up on the mule's slippery wet back proved almost impossible. Using the rifle as a cane, muzzle upward, he latched onto Ruby's tail with his other hand, and she blazed them a trail back home—and right up onto their little front porch. Geraldine finally stopped yelping, and the cold winter night became silent once again.

****

Emmy threw more wood on the fire, and then sat on the bed beside her husband. "I never believed in my heart that you were gone. And my prayers were answered, you're safe now."

"No thanks to Yancy." Caleb took a big gulp of coffee, and wolfed down the last piece of bread with a spoonful of stew. "He wasn't my friend after all." The anger in his voice spoke volumes. "It was rough times living and working in the goldfields, Emmy. Harder even than farming. But thoughts of you kept me going, and after months and months and months our luck changed. We found a little side creek where the panning was good. Then it played out, and Yancy went plumb crazy. I caught him one night stealing all the gold and making ready to take off. We fought, and he hit me in the head with a rock and left me for dead."

Emmy removed the empty coffee cup and soup bowl before she reached for Caleb's hand. "My heart near breaks at the thought of what you went through, all to give me a better life—when all I ever wanted was you."

"I realize that now, Emmy".

"But why were you out in the blizzard? And what about my receiving your *just in case* letter?"

"For the last few months, I've been working my way back home. When I reached Kansas, I had just enough money left to take the stage to our nearby town. I figured I could hoof it from there to our house before the storm hit. I was wrong about that too. And as far as the letter goes, Yancy knew I carried it with me. I'm guessing he sent it to you so you wouldn't come looking for me—or for him. Another miner found me and saved my life. It was all for nothing, Emmy. I lost the gold and worse yet, the years I could have spent with you."

"We'll be together from now on. That's all that matters."

Emmy got up and burned the dreaded letter. She didn't need a reminder of how close she came to losing Caleb. Then she lay down beside her husband, and he held her tight.

"I love you, Caleb."

"I love you too, Emmy."

With a sigh, she snuggled closer. Her wait was over. Caleb was home.

Wings of Fire
by

Jana Richards

July 1943

William Crane banked his Harvard hard to the left and grinned as the brilliant yellow of the plane's wing sparkled in the prairie sunshine. The land below spread out like a patchwork quilt of multi-colored squares, divided in half by the muddy river cutting a path through the fields. Will marveled at the vastness of his new temporary home. He turned the plane in a slow circle. In every direction, the land stretched to the horizon. Only the low-slung buildings of the city of Saskatoon a couple of miles away marred the illusion of a never-ending ocean of land.

Tiny Saskatoon, Saskatchewan couldn't be more different from the home he'd left in England. London teemed with people and noise and excitement, whereas life in his current posting moved at a far more sedate pace, even during wartime. But the biggest difference was that Saskatoon's buildings still stood whole, its people blissfully unaware of the terror of German bombs in the night.

Will gritted his teeth, barely restraining the urge to slap his fist hard against the cockpit. Damn it, he should be back in England, fighting for his country. Instead he was here, meandering across the Canadian prairies.

He clamped down on his impatience. He needed to be here. Without the training he was receiving with the British Commonwealth Air Training Plan, and without earning his wings, he wouldn't be of much use to the

Royal Air Force. His time to fight would come.

Still, frustration ate at him. Below, he saw a farmer working his land next to a tree-lined farmyard. Will's spirits lifted. Time for a bit of fun.

Gradually he reduced the altitude of the Harvard. By the time he buzzed the farmer on his tractor, Will could almost reach down and shake the man's hand. He laughed as the farmer shook his fist at the bright yellow plane.

Will's amusement was short-lived. Flying low was a stupid, reckless thing to do, and strictly forbidden. Every training plane had a number painted on its side in bold, black letters. All the farmer had to do was report the number to the RCMP who in turn would report it to the Air Force. He'd be sent packing immediately, as an example of recklessness to the other student pilots. Will sobered at the thought. He was too damned close to getting his wings to wash out now.

He pulled up to gain altitude and made a starboard turn, preparing to head back to base. Suddenly the engine sputtered, and oil sprayed onto the windscreen in front of him, obscuring his vision. The Harvard rapidly lost altitude. He was going down.

Will's mind worked furiously as he prepared to crash-land. He'd practiced forced landings, both solo and with his instructors, on runways and on grass fields. But this was the first time a forced landing was for real, with the safety of his plane and his life in the balance.

Months of training took over as he calmly planned. He needed to land in an open space, away from buildings or ditches. And most important, he needed to keep the plane upright. If it nosedived into the dirt, he'd break a propeller or possibly a wing. If he destroyed a training plane because of his stupid stunt, he'd be washed out for sure.

There was a pasture behind the farmer's barn that looked level and free of rocks. If he could make it there, he might just have a chance.

No such luck.

The plane was losing altitude faster than he'd anticipated. He skimmed over the tractor once more, grimacing as the farmer jumped from his seat and flattened himself to the earth beneath the machine. A large haystack loomed in front of him. The plane's wheels hit the uneven ground, bouncing once, twice. Will was thrown forward, his jaw smacking against the control panel with a painful, bone-jarring knock. He braked hard and steered to the left. The right wing brushed the haystack, knocking over the loose hay. Will held his breath as the Harvard teetered on one wheel. Then it bounced back onto both wheels and wheezed to a stall.

For a few moments the only sounds Will heard were the squawks of frightened chickens as they flew in a hundred different directions. He ran a hand over his jaw. It was sore and would likely turn a nasty black and blue, but he didn't think it was broken. The rest of him seemed to be largely unhurt as well.

Will eased himself from the cockpit and jumped out, taking stock of the situation. Despite the way he'd landed, the Harvard sustained minimal damage. But a blown tire and the problem with the engine meant there was no way he could fly it back to base. Will sighed. How was he going to get back? And how was he going to explain this one to his commander?

The farmer approached him on the run. Will braced

himself for the tongue lashing he was sure would follow, knowing he deserved every bit of the man's wrath. As the farmer came closer, the wind blew off a wide-brimmed hat, releasing a cascade of auburn curls that glowed like fire in the sun. Will stared in astonishment, his jaw hanging slack. The farmer was a woman. A very beautiful woman. Even the baggy overalls and scuffed work boots couldn't diminish her attractiveness.

"Are you all right?" she asked when she reached him. "Are you hurt?"

Will rubbed his sore jaw once more, his eyes never leaving her face. She had the fair complexion of a redhead, with a sprinkling of freckles peppering her nose and cheeks. Her eyes were an unusual mixture of blue and green, which were currently filled with concern for him.

"Yes, thank you, I'm fine. Just a few bruises, I believe."

"Good. Then I can do this." She let fly with a hard right to his shoulder.

Will staggered back a pace, taken off guard. "Steady on!" he said, massaging his shoulder. For a small woman she packed an amazingly big punch. "What did you do that for?"

"You're one of those pilots from the air school, aren't you?" She jabbed at his chest with a pointed finger. Her eyes, previously full of concern, now blazed with fury. "I'm sick to death of you crazy idiots dive-bombing my farm and scaring the animals. That haystack represents this winter's feed for my livestock, and you nearly destroyed it. I wish you'd all go back where you came from."

Months of frustration and anger he'd kept carefully

under wraps suddenly unleashed itself. Will grabbed her hands to stop her incessant jabbing, pulling her against him. He snarled into her upturned face.

"I'd love to go back where I came from, miss. I'd give anything to go back to my old life. The only problem is that where I came from no longer exists. The Nazis made sure of that."

She stared up at him, her mouth slightly open and forming a little O. She was so close that Will could count the freckles across the bridge of her nose and smell the scent of soap and tractor grease on her skin. In an instant her gaze shifted from anger and defiance to empathy.

"I'm so sorry," she whispered. "I can't imagine losing my home."

Having her pressed so close caused his body to respond even as his heart made a painful lurch. It had been a long time since a woman had looked at him that way, as if she could see beyond the uniform to truly understand the man underneath.

He realized with a start that he clenched her hands in a sort of death grip, pressed tight against his chest. He let go abruptly and took a step back, wondering if she had felt the hammering of his heart.

Will cleared his throat. "I apologize, miss, for everything. It was stupid of me to buzz you on the tractor and inexcusable to ruin your haystack." He glanced at the partly collapsed stack. "Perhaps I can help you set it to rights?"

Before she could form an answer, an older man limped out of the nearby barn.

"Evie, Evie! Are you all right? I heard a crash!"

"I'm fine, Dad," she called.

The old man stopped short when he saw the airplane

next to the haystack. "What the blazes happened here?"

Will opened his mouth to tell the old farmer the truth, but before he could say anything, the young woman spoke up.

"The pilot had engine trouble, Dad."

Will stared at her, astonished. She could so easily tell her father about the low dive he'd made at her. Why was she doing this? He caught her almost imperceptible wink.

"There's no real harm done, and the pilot here—"

"Leading Aircraftman William Crane," he supplied.

"—Leading Aircraftman Crane has offered to restack the hay. Isn't that right, sir?"

He nearly burst out laughing at the look of wide-eyed innocence she gave him. Something lifted in his heart, something that had been lying dormant inside him for so long he almost didn't recognize it.

Hope.

A grin tugged at his mouth. All these months he'd felt the only reason he was still alive was to fight for his country. He'd never expected to find a purpose beyond that, and had never expected a future beyond the war. Who knew he'd find a reason for living just outside of Saskatoon?

****

Author's Note

The British Commonwealth Air Training Plan (BCATP) 1939 – 1945:

When war broke out in Europe in September 1939, leaders like Winston Churchill knew that this war would be won or lost in the air. By December 1939, an agreement had been made between Canada, Britain, Australia, and New Zealand, which called for Canada to train these countries' air crews. Canada's wide-open spaces and distance from the fighting made it an ideal training ground for new pilots. Though Canada administered the Plan and picked up most of the costs, most graduates went on to serve in Britain's Royal Air Force. At its peak, the Plan maintained two hundred and thirty-one training sites, including one in Saskatoon, Saskatchewan. It trained pilots, navigators, bomb aimers, radio operators, air gunners, and flight engineers. Roughly half of the 131,553 graduates came from Britain, Australia, and New Zealand. For many of these young men, it was their first time away from home.

A Lark

by

Gabbi Grey

Shelby was not known for her patience, and today had been all kinds of trying for her. Glancing at her watch for the millionth time, she groaned. A whole three minutes had passed. Next, she checked the incoming flight section. Lark's plane had landed nine minutes ago, so where was she? Where were all the passengers?

Someone nudged her shoulder, and she was prepared to snap, but she recognized Jana. Their gazes met.

Jana grinned. "Impatient much?"

"It's been two months." Shelby growled the words, unable to hide her frustration.

Jana rubbed her protruding belly, huge under the tent of a dress. "If they were delayed by even a few days, Gary was likely to miss the birth."

Shelby winced. Yeah, she didn't have it as bad as some. "It's great he'll make it."

"They've scheduled the Caesarian for Tuesday. I wanted natural, but after the mess of the last birth, my doctor said C-section was safer."

She believed in safety, but entirely too much information had just been shared, so Shelby simply nodded.

"Oh." On a sharp inhalation Jana grabbed Shelby's hand and pressed it to her belly.

The movement jarred. "Was that a kick or a contraction?" Having never placed a hand on a pregnant woman's belly before, Shelby was clueless.

"Kick." Jana's radiant smile would have lit a dark room. "She's going to be a soccer player, I swear. Oh, you can coach her."

Well, there was that. Teaching French at the local high school left Shelby two periods short of a full class load, and never one to lose an opportunity, their principal had tapped Shelby to coach several different teams including, but not limited to, soccer, baseball, lacrosse, and volleyball, plus hockey in the winter. Well, assistant coach of hockey. Their girls' team was amazing, but Coach Wannock relegated Shelby to physical training while he stuck to strategy. That suited her just fine. She understood hockey well enough, but she wouldn't want the responsibility for line changes and position selection.

Ironically, Shelby wasn't known for her fitness. Oh, she could run a few laps and kick a ball around, but her strength lay in encouraging young women to succeed in sports. Lark was a whole other story. Shelby's partner of five years was at the peak of physical fitness and worked out every day she wasn't on shift. Shelby was exhausted just being a spectator of Lark's grueling workout schedule. Of course, with her job, Lark had to be in top physical shape.

"They're here."

Jana's excited exclamation had Shelby snapping her head up.

Gary was the first one through the gate. He spotted Jana, pushed his cart with all his gear aside, and swept his wife into a huge hug.

The belly bump got in the way somewhat, but they managed, kissing with an exuberance Shelby envied.

"Hey, you."

At Lark's deep and rumbling voice, Shelby turned, dismayed she'd missed her lover's arrival. Part of her longed to take Lark in her arms and kiss her senseless, but the part of her that still worried about being *out* in public held her back. The disappointment in Lark's eyes was momentary, but it was there. The argument was as old as their relationship. Lark was out and proud. People knew she spent all her spare time with Shelby. Therefore, Shelby was probably a lesbian as well. Hell, likely no one in town believed they were just roommates, but Shelby kept up the pretense, in the process hurting Lark's feelings.

Man up. Or in this case, woman *up.*

Holding open her arms, Shelby waited for Lark to step into her embrace, which she did, posthaste. God, it felt so good to be clinging like this. Two months away wasn't that long; that's what she kept telling herself. Military deployments went on much longer and with just as much threat of danger. Still, saying and believing were two different things.

Tears stung her eyes as she buried her face against Lark's neck. There was almost half a foot difference in height between them, and Shelby wasn't all that short.

Lark topped out at an inch under six feet and carried herself tall and proud.

She had confidence to spare while Shelby struggled constantly with self-doubts.

"I missed you, Shel."

Lark's arms were tight around her, making breathing a challenge. But there was no better feeling in the world, so she held on.

"M.L., we're, uh, leaving."

Lark pulled away, still sheltering Shelby. "Pleasure

working with you, Captain."

"Hopefully, not again for a while. I'm thinking July or August."

"I hope you're right."

Lark's voice was strained, and although Shelby couldn't see Captain Raymond, she sensed the tall and imposing man behind her. She should turn and greet Lark's sometimes boss, but she just didn't have it in her. When the captain and his cart departed, she pulled back. "They still calling you M.L.?"

Now Lark's grin was back. "Better short for Meadow Lark than some of the other names they could come up with." She placed a finger on Shelby's brow. "Not what you're thinking. They're good men, Shel. Men I've served with for years. They respect me and know I'll do a good job."

"I know." And she did. But when the job was as dangerous as Lark's, the other men having her back was crucial. "Several guys died, though, right?"

"None on our crew. We all made it back safe and sound. Now, can we please get out of this airport? We had a four-hour layover at LAX, and I'm exhausted."

"Twenty-two hours of traveling will do that."

"I know, right?" Lark yawned. "And it's almost the same time that I left, and the same day, and I know there's a logical explanation—"

"International Date Line."

"—but it just doesn't make sense to me."

"But you're home now, and that's what matters." And it was. It'd take time for Lark to reacclimate to being back, but she'd manage. She had before and she would again.

"I love my job, but I hate being away."

Shelby missed her like crazy as well but would never stand in the way. Lark had every right to make her own decisions, and even if that meant putting herself in harm's way, she was bound and determined to do it. Her fearless warrior.

"I was planning to take you out for dinner, but if you're too tired, we can head home, and I'll make something simple."

Lark's blue eyes sparkled. "I'm hankering for some pasta. Really good pasta."

"Like Gregory's?"

"Exactly like Gregory's."

There were few fancy restaurants in Prince George, but Gregory's was unique. They served everything from steak and potatoes to pasta to Greek to Chinese. A wide menu for every taste. Perhaps a little on the pricey side, but Shelby was more than willing to fork over the money if it made Lark happy.

"You stow your bags in the SUV, and I'll call and make sure they have a table ready." She didn't foresee too many people there at two o'clock on a Sunday afternoon, but she wasn't going to chance it.

The first set of automatic doors swished open, and a blast of hot air met the women. The second set opened to the outside, and Lark shuddered. "Mother of God, does it have to be this cold?"

Shelby managed not to roll her eyes, but it was a close thing. Lark's complaints about the cold were legendary. "You live in central British Columbia in Canada in the middle of winter. You were expecting balmy conditions?"

Lark shot her a glare. "It was nearly forty degrees Celsius when we left Sydney."

A sobering reminder, if she needed one.

"Well, it's nearly forty *below* here with the windchill." Shelby took charge, pushing the cart to the parking lot. Last night's snow had been cleared, so the path was easy to navigate. She wore her parka, zero-rated boots, a hat, and gloves. She'd been sweating in the airport but had known the cold was coming.

Lark also wore her parka and boots, but her jacket was still open.

"Honey, do up your coat." Shelby didn't like to nag, but it came naturally. She was the same with her students.

Lark obeyed, and as Shelby took her backpack, Lark hefted her suitcase into the trunk. They both knew Shelby could have done it, but Lark didn't need as much time to prepare. Nope, the woman just hefted and in went the bag. Like she was lifting a feather rather than a twenty-five-pound bag.

"I'll drive, you call Gregory's."

Shelby handed over the keys and rounded to the passenger side. Heaving herself up, she landed in the passenger seat. After she'd secured her seat belt, she yanked off her gloves, found the restaurant in her contact list, and dialed.

"Gregory's, how may I assist you?"

"Anton? It's Shelby."

"Ah, are you on your way?"

"I am."

"Everything's ready."

Little butterflies exploded in her belly. "Be there in ten."

"Perfect."

Hanging up, she placed her phone back in her

pocket. Glancing up, she met Lark's gaze.

"You already pay for parking?"

"Yep, we're good. Anton's saving us a table."

Lark's grin was wide. "You know, I may be craving sleep, but mushroom fettuccini sounds perfect."

Shelby detested anything that grew in, uh, well…mushrooms didn't cut it for her. "I'm thinking about dolmades." She glanced over at Lark who was looking at her dubiously. "Well, I really want steak and shrimp, but that's bad for the environment because of belching cows and—"

"It's not every day I come home, babe. If you want steak, have steak. We'll go vegetarian the rest of the week." Which was always quite a feat given the cost of fresh produce during the winter. There were plenty of protein substitutes out there.

"But you'll need the protein." Did she sound like she was whining? Maybe. Just a bit.

"Shel, I'm not on shift until Wednesday, and I'm only doing light workouts between now and then. You remember that Angus works right alongside me, and he's vegan?"

Blech. Just the thought of giving up cheese, yogurt, and milk pained her greatly. A little meat was a small sacrifice.

"Okay, I'll have the steak." And feel guilty for days but man, it'd be worth it.

Pulling the SUV into a parking space, Lark cut the engine.

Shelby was reaching for the door handle when Lark placed a hand on her arm, stilling her. Turning to meet her lover's gaze, Shelby sucked in a breath at the intensity she met.

"I really missed you, Shel. More than I can say."

Goddamn, no more tears. "I missed you too. Skype is great, but having you here is better." Never mind that there'd been only two Skype sessions and half a dozen calls over the whole two months. Lark had been on the front lines for most of that time with little rest. When she had time off, she tended to crash, sleep for hours, inhale some food, then go right back to sleep. Shelby understood, but it didn't stop her from wanting more contact.

Lark leaned toward her, and Shelby met her halfway. Their kiss was sweet. Just a light peck of lips. Something akin to a promise. Pulling back, she opened her eyes. "I love you, you know."

"I do." Lark opened her door. "But I'm starving."

Within moments they were through the door of the restaurant, assailed by all the wonderful smells Shelby associated with this establishment.

Anton greeted them like long lost friends and escorted them to their table. "Welcome home, our hero."

Blushing furiously, Lark shot Shelby a look.

She shrugged. "The newspapers carried the story. I didn't say anything."

"And the meal is on the house, so order whatever you want."

Both Shelby and Lark started to argue, but Anton held up his hands. "See, I own the place, so I get to make the rules." He eyed the women. "Mushroom fettuccini with extra garlic bread and house salad to start?"

Lark nodded.

"Steak—medium, baked potato, and Caesar salad?"

Shelby nodded, albeit reluctantly.

"And chocolate mousse for dessert."

Already tasting the creamy chocolate, Shelby nodded again.

"Good, I'll be back with a bottle of red." Then he was gone.

The two women gazed at each other and laughed. "I think we come here a lot, don't we?"

"At least twice a month for almost five years." Lark's grin widened. "I don't think we've changed our order more than half a dozen times in all those years."

"Like an old married couple."

Crap.

"Well, you know, like, uh…"

Lark pressed a discreet hand to Shelby's thigh. "I knew what you meant."

That touch meant everything. Although meant only to reassure, there was a promise of more. The reminder that although they'd endured separations before, and likely would again, the reunion was always sweet, tender, and sometimes frantic and frenetic.

Focus.

"How bad was it?" She didn't want to know, but this was part of the job. Part of being Lark's support network.

"People have died, Shel. Mostly at the beginning before we got there, though. No one died on our watch—other firefighters or civilians."

"That's good, right?"

Lark's half-shrug said it all. "The animals who died…Shel, it broke my heart. There was nothing we could do for them. Our job was mitigation. Get in there, build the fire lines, prevent the spread, deal with the hot spots, then move on."

Pretty much what she always did. "I heard about the heat."

Taking a large gulp of water, Lark nodded. "Yeah. Again, temperatures I've almost never encountered. The forest fires here aren't as bad, and down in California there's almost always wind. Wind is destructive, but it keeps the worst of the heat at bay." She waited while Anton poured two glasses of wine, leaving the bottle on the table. "We were swapped out by another Canadian crew."

Dread overwhelmed. "Are you going back?"

"Not likely. Their fire season is almost half over. By rotation time, they may not need our help."

"I can't wrap my mind around the size of the fires."

"I know, right?" Lark twirled her water glass. "I was presented with one fire line. One miniscule piece in a giant puzzle. Not even a speck. And at times it felt futile, like what we were doing didn't make any difference."

"Lark—"

"But then we'd save a town or rescue a few animals, and I'd remember why I became a firefighter in the first place. I also did a few EMS calls, so that helped in feeling needed."

Shelby hated hearing about the painful side of the job. The buildings they couldn't save, the people they couldn't rescue. They lived on a major highway, so there were plenty of crashes. Lark was trained in extractions. Hell, she was trained in just about every kind of rescue possible, as well as her paramedic training. She was one of the most qualified members of the crew. And the hardest working. She took all the overtime shifts. All the crap shifts. They hadn't had a single Christmas Day together yet, but Shelby willingly made those sacrifices because it made Lark happy. The woman loved her job as much as she loved life. As much as she loved Shelby.

Or so Shelby hoped.

Before she could ask another question, Anton arrived with their food. With profuse thanks, the women accepted their meals and settled down to eat.

Shelby had managed toast for breakfast, but nerves had prevented her from eating more, and that'd been about eight hours ago. "You're hungry too, eh?" Her lover had consumed almost half her meal.

"Airline food is not the best. They upgraded the team to first class, but the food was still, uh…"

If they'd been home, the vulgarity would've come naturally, but Lark was always circumspect in public. "I get the picture."

"They fed us well in Australia as well, but there's something about coming home. The food tastes better."

"Maybe it's the company." See, she could flirt.

"Definitely the company." Lark tapped her index finger to her lips.

Shelby poured another glass of wine for Lark but switched to water for herself since she was driving. The snow had started to fall, and there was a storm warning in effect. They'd be fine as long as they headed out soon.

"How was the meal?" Anton had come upon them quietly.

Lark placed a hand on her stomach. "Amazing, as always."

"Yes, it was delicious. Our compliments to the chef."

"I'll tell her. Always good to stroke her ego." He leaned in conspiratorially. "And to pay her well."

"Which is why we should pay for our food."

This free meal thing was sticking in Lark's craw. Shelby didn't blame her. The woman hated being seen as heroic. She was doing her job—nothing more and nothing less. She'd worked damn hard to be considered an equal to her male colleagues, and they saw her as such. But a whole bunch of them were older than Lark's twenty-nine, and they were protective of her. Nothing pissed her off more than that.

Anton shrugged. "I'll wrap up the leftovers and bring your mousse."

"With an offer like that, it's hard to stay mad." Shelby cut Lark a warning look, and although her mouth twisted in annoyance, Lark held her tongue.

With another flourish, Anton was off.

"I think he's laughing at us." Lark did not look amused.

"No, I think he's cheering for us."

"It would serve him right if we never came…cheering?" She arched an eyebrow. "Shel, why would Anton be cheering for us?"

"Well, cheering for me." God, she was going to do this. She was really going to do this.

Pulling the velvet box from her bag, she moved as gracefully as possible to one knee.

Yep, she was really doing this.

"Lark, you're my everything."

"Shel—"

"Don't or I won't get through this speech, and it took me a long time to write and memorize, so just…"

"I won't say a word." Her eyes shimmered.

"Like I said, uh, you're my everything. For five years you've shared my life, and I haven't let you celebrate that. Well, that ends tonight. I want to be yours, just like I want you to be mine. I want us to get married and have a dog and—"

Lark let out a very unladylike squeal.

Whether at the married part or the dog part, Shelby wasn't sure. "But I need you in my life, and I'm willing to tell the world. Or at least our little corner of it." Now she opened the ring box. The engagement ring she'd chosen was simple with a single diamond. Lark could never wear it at work, but when they were together, it would sit proudly on her finger.

If she said yes.

Lark held her hand against her mouth. Yet she said nothing. No nod, no "Yes," just…nothing.

"Uh, my old knees won't be able to hold me up much longer." Okay, so Shelby was thirty-five, and her knees weren't causing her too much pain, but her heart was going to beat out of her chest, given the stress.

"So I can speak now?"

Oh, right.

Lark wasn't covering her mouth out of emotion, but to hold back laughter.

Well, damn.

"Yes, woman, you can speak." Shelby didn't hide the exasperation in her voice. She'd set this up, but now the suspense was killing her.

"Well, the answer is *yes*. Yes today, yes tomorrow, and yes for the rest of our lives. As long as you're willing to put up with my crazy job, I'm all for marriage." Lark took the ring box and placed it on the table. Then she rose, holding out her hands to Shelby.

With much gratitude, Shelby accepted the help and allowed herself to be pulled up.

Relief.

Lark removed the ring from its velvet home and held it out to Shelby. "Will you do the honors?"

"Gladly." Her hand might've shaken a bit, but she managed to slide the ring on, and it fit perfectly. That was remarkable because she rarely got things right the first time.

Stroking Lark's cheek with her hand, Shelby encouraged the taller woman to angle her head down so they could kiss. Their first proper out-of-the-closet kiss. While Shelby would've been happy to keep it chaste, Lark deepened it. The kiss became hot, dark, and possessive.

Mine.

Hers.

Shelby had no issue with giving herself over both to the passion and the possession. She loved with her whole heart, and nothing, not even the biggest fire in history, would stop her from making Lark hers. Permanently.

The applause, though, pulled her back into the moment. She opened her eyes and gazed into Lark's. "I guess we have an audience."

"I'll show you proper appreciation once we get home." There was a promise of more in those eyes.

"And now you have mousse." Anton held the two bowls aloft with a wide grin on his face.

"Ah, so that's the cheering." Lark helped Shelby into her chair and then sat. "He knew?"

"He did." Shelby'd needed to be accountable to someone. He'd have pushed her and not let her chicken out.

"And if I'd wanted to go home?"

"Then it would've been a very different proposal."

"Ah, good, then." Lark held her hand out so she could inspect the ring. "This is perfect."

"And the animal shelter is waiting for us. They have

three dogs we might want to adopt."

"Only three?"

Damn, walked into that one.

"We're only adopting one."

"We'll see."

The next day they adopted all three.

But not until the next day.

Apple Crisp
by

Terry Graham

"Sidney!"

Six-year-old Sid's head snapped up, his knobby knees still shaking, and he swiped at his cheeks. Hot, wet tears trickled down his chin, but he ignored them. All around, dark shadows hovered closer and he sniffled. A musty, sweet smell drifted over him—one he hadn't smelled in a while. Apples. His mouth watered, but his throat tightened. He loved apples. And apple crisp. His mom made the best apple crisp and always gave him an extra big helping. Unless he was bad.

Try as he might, another tear trickled out.

From farther away, Nana called his name, and another voice rumbled, too faint to make out.

As he moved, something tickled his neck. He jumped, swatting at the spot. Thin, sticky strands wrapped his knuckles and he hurled it off. Spiders scared him. Even the story of the spider on a farm, that Mom used to read when he was little, didn't help. All those tiny legs and the way they dropped on you when you weren't looking was creepy. With a shiver, he tucked himself into the corner, hoping they'd leave him alone.

If he was lucky, everybody would leave him alone.

He squeezed his eyes shut and dropped his head.

A footstep thudded, and the floor trembled, then another, and another. Slow heavy steps that moved away. Too heavy to be Nana's.

Whoever it was, they wouldn't find him.

His breath caught. What if the fire was back? Was that why they were yelling?

69

It didn't matter. He deserved to die. Wanted to even.

Another sob ripped through him, but his throat hurt so bad no sound came out.

Would they even care? They hadn't cared when Momma died. He still saw them, standing around her grave, staring as the men shoveled dry, red dirt into the hole. No one even cried. They'd come home and pretended nothing had happened, eating and drinking while he sat on the couch, too sad to even eat. Some of them even laughed.

They said they loved Momma, but they didn't even miss her.

His name floated through the air again. Closer, but still too far away to recognize. They wouldn't find him. No one used the old mud porch anymore.

He swallowed another sob and cocked his head. Nana Lucy never hollered. Not even the time he'd broken the vase Grandpa had given her.

He'd never said anything as horrible to Nana before though.

The words rang in his head, louder even than the fires that had raged past the house two days before, and another torrent of hate choked his throat. *Ugly! Stupid! Mean!* How had he said those things? He loved Nana.

Lately, he'd been saying lots of things he didn't mean.

His body shook again, all the trapped sadness bubbling up, burning his throat and eyes, forcing its way out. Through the storm of tears, voices washed over him. Nana's, as quiet as the wind that whispered outside at night, and another. Deeper and slow, the noise threaded through the darkness like Nana's sewing. And footsteps. Heavy thudding footsteps that shook the whole house.

He shuddered and hugged his knees tighter. It was probably just Mr. Mason. He liked Mr. Mason. He came every day. Pa had asked him to check on them, but Mr. Mason brought Nana flowers sometimes. He liked Nana. Maybe even loved her.

Not like him. No one loved him anymore.

"Sidney?" The door creaked open, and a sliver of light shone through the crack.

"Pa?" Sidney had to suck in a breath to get the word out, too surprised to move.

The thudding echoed faster as his father hurried into the room.

Why was Pa here? He was fighting the horrible fires. Every night, he and Nana watched them on the news. Scary, monster fires that ate everything around them. Every night his throat got tighter and tighter as he tried not to cry.

"Come out here, son." His father stopped inside the door, his head outlined in the brightness as he lifted a hand and brushed away a cobweb. Bigger than most of his friends' fathers, Pa reminded him sometimes of a superhero, especially when he had his ax in his hand, except Pa was smarter and had to go to work all the time.

"I…I can't."

"Can't? Or won't?"

The sickness in his stomach crawled up and choked him, but he fought the sour taste down. "Won't, I guess." His fist rubbed his face. Pa always knew when he'd done wrong. He didn't know how, but somehow, he always did.

"Is it because you yelled at Nana?" The light blinded Sid as his father dropped to sit on a stool. A yellow helmet spun on the floor, followed by the familiar sucking sound as he ripped open his jacket. "She said you called her some nasty names."

Sid's shoulders collapsed. He'd always been small, smaller than the other boys, even though his Pa was big, but he'd never felt this tiny. "I didn't mean it." One word, *bitch*, he didn't even understand. The older boys at school had used the word and it sounded bad, so he'd screamed it.

He buried his head in his knees again, but Nana's stricken face wouldn't go away. Her face had crumbled, like pie crust when crushed in his little hand. That had scared him too, because she looked like Mom, only older, with white hair instead of the sunny color of Mom's.

"Why don't you come out here and we'll discuss it? See if there isn't some way to fix things?" Pa shifted, his pants crinkling, and patted a box. Filled with the jars Mom had used to make jam, the box hadn't been moved in so long a cloud of dust billowed in the stillness.

A wriggle of hope let Sid lever himself up, but his legs wobbled. His hand clutched the edge of the empty barrel. He wished it still held a wrinkled apple or two. He hadn't eaten an apple since Mom died. First because he wasn't hungry, then later because they were hard to find. Nana said the fires had eaten all the apple trees.

The hand stretched out, palm upward. "Come on. Nothing's so bad it can't be fixed."

He wasn't sure about that, but if anyone could fix what he'd done, Pa could, so he reached out. Heat wrapped around his fingers and trickled up his arm as he shuffled out.

"Nana's really mad." Pa would be too, when he found out what he'd done. As much as he wanted, all he could do was stare at the floor. If he faced Pa he'd see the sad, hollow emptiness he'd seen ever since Mom died.

"She says you smashed some pictures. And ripped up some books."

"Yeah." Even now, he wanted to kick the floor. He didn't have the strength though. The demon that ate at him every day refused to go away. He'd tried to send it away by busting the picture, but nothing helped.

When Pa reached out and brushed his hair back, the anger kicked up again. He swatted the hand away.

"Hey, now." Two strong arms wrapped around him and pulled him close. He fought back, but his arms were too tired, his legs too shaky from crouching in the dark, and the loneliness too hungry. He buried his face in his father's chest and sobbed, his body shuddering to not give in, and failing. "It's okay, son. Let it out." Hands smoothed his back, the same way Mom's used to, and tucked him into a lap. It wasn't Mom's lap. Pa's legs were too hard and hot, like the stovetop before it cooled, almost too hot to bear, but being held felt good. So good all the bad feelings shoved and clawed and boiled away, like the spaghetti water when Nana forgot to shut off the burner. They bubbled up so fast he didn't even try to swallow them. He held on with all his might, hands clutching the edges of the jacket and tried not to let go. The voice was different too, as Pa's rumble murmured against his ear. "That's it, baby. Let it all out."

"I'm not a baby." He pushed against the chest, but not hard. Six-year-olds weren't supposed to cry, and they weren't babies, but they weren't supposed to have tantrums either.

"I know you aren't." A kiss landed on the back of

his head. "You're my big boy." His father's chest expanded, and he sniffled. "But you promised to take care of Nana for me. That means doing as she says, doesn't it?"

His head scraped at Pa's chest as he nodded, and his nose crinkled. Pa smelled of smoke and that stuff he used under his arms, and sweat, like after he'd worked in the sun. Sid inhaled and a bit of the fear disappeared.

"So, what happened?"

The sour hurt swirled in his tummy again, and Sid burrowed against the thick, cotton shirt. "Didn't Nana tell you?"

"She did." A finger chucked his chin and forced him to face Pa. Dark brown eyes glistened, tired looking with tiny red cobwebs. "But I want to you to tell me."

He swallowed hard, but the sickness stayed. "I wanted to watch a movie. She told me no." She'd said he had to wait until after dinner.

One brow rose and Pa's lips tightened. Sid stared at the sweat stain spreading across his father's shirt, an ugly white line twisting around a darker green. "She said I had to finish my dinner. But I didn't want to." Every time he took a bite, his stomach cramped. "So, I asked if I could call you."

The scariness had followed him the whole day, even when he crawled under the bed. Nana told him people couldn't breathe and that's why they died in fires, and that's how he felt every day. Like his chest wouldn't work. Like Mom, buried under the dirt. His voice quivered. "She said no. You're too busy."

Too busy. Too busy to talk. Too busy to come home. Too busy saving people.

Pa's arms snuggled him, like Mom used to do, and

his voice shook too. "You know I want to talk to you all the time, don't you? That no one means more to me than you and Nana? But I have an important job, and sometimes that means I can't. You're big enough to understand that."

Sid pulled away at the reminder. He didn't want to be big enough.

"She made me eat peas." *Peas!* The most disgusting vegetable in the world.

For a minute, he thought Pa would bellow in that voice he used when the pigs got out. Then a slow rumbling began, and his father hugged him again. "She's worried about you. We both are. You're wasting away since your Mom died. How do you expect to grow up as strong as those superheroes if you don't eat?"

He shrugged as the momentary comfort faded away. His dad was a superhero. Mom had told him that every day when Pa put on his yellow outfit and left. She'd get sad and worried and watch the news every night instead of paying attention to him. Sometimes he'd hear her crying in bed, when Pa didn't call every day. But that was a secret, she said, because Pa had more important worries. She'd be crying every night if she was still alive. Cause Pa almost never called lately.

"I was mad." The secret slid out like the brown snake Mom had beaten to death after it slithered from beneath the sofa. "So, I threw the picture."

"The one of me and Mom?"

He nodded, so ashamed he wanted to curl back up in the corner. Once he'd started throwing things, the badness told him to keep going. First, he hurled the picture, then the remote, then anything in reach. Nana had tried to take the book away, the ones with the fairy tales Mom liked best, but he'd screamed those words at her and kicked her shin, then run away.

"Can you tell me why?"

Sid stilled and watched the dust dance in the surrounding light. The mud room was cramped and dark, covered in layers of dirt. He'd come here to hide, to cry.

"Because I miss her." Even saying it took every bit of courage he had. He wasn't supposed to miss her. He was six, a little man. He wasn't supposed to cry or get mad. He was supposed to be brave like Pa.

"I miss her too." Pa's hand cupped his cheek, his rough thumb wiping a path through the wetness. "I miss her every minute of every day."

"You do?"

"Of course." His father's forehead wrinkled. "Why would you think I don't?"

"You never talk about her." Sid's lip trembled. He wanted to talk about her, but every time he tried, his eyes prickled, and his stomach hurt.

Pa nodded, a strange cramped smile on his face, then he pulled Sid close and leaned his chin on top of his head. "I was trying to make it easier on you." The stool creaked as his father started rocking him. "I see now that was a mistake. I didn't want you to think you had to talk about her if you don't want to. But we should."

"We should?" All his life, Pa had said he talked too much.

"We should. Because we should never forget her. And talking about her keeps her alive. In here." Pa wrapped his hand up in his much larger one and bumped them against both their chests.

The light streaming through the door crept closer to the barrel and Sid inhaled. "Did you cry?" The very thought frightened him, that his big strong dad could cry.

"I did. I cried a lot the first few days. After I put you to bed. It gets easier though. After a few good cries, it hurts less and you remember the good things. Like how your mom would sing when she vacuumed, and how she'd laugh at my bad jokes."

Sid peered up suspiciously. Pa's jokes were funny and when they weren't Mom's laugh was. But remembering made him miss her more.

"It's okay to cry, son, and it's good that you want to talk about her. But it's not all right that you disrespected Nana."

Sid's stomach lurched, and all the bad feelings came back. "I know." Nana might never love him again. Who would take care of him if she didn't? And what if Pa died too?

He threw himself against Pa's chest. Thump, thump, thump, the blood pounded as fast as a kangaroo running. Was the beat from his heart or Pa's? "Do you have to go away again, Pa?" He hated whining like a baby, but when Pa stroked his head, he decided he didn't care.

"I wish I didn't, but I do."

"Why?" Why couldn't he stay home? With him? Why did Mr. Mason have to watch over them?

Pa's chest expanded, so wide Sid's arms slipped. He lifted Sid and set on the ground. "You know how we feel about Mom?" he asked, looking tired and sad. "How much we miss her?" Sid nodded though he didn't want to admit it. "I have to make sure no one else has to feel like that. I have an important job, one few people can do. And it's your job to make sure I don't have to worry about you and Nana. You can do that, can't you?"

Sid stared at the floor. His feet looked tiny next to

Pa's. "I don't want to."

"I know you don't. But sometimes we have to do things we don't like. Like eating our peas so Nana won't worry or going to bed so we're rested the next day."

Sid pressed his lips together. Was that why Mom only cried at night? So Pa wouldn't worry? He wasn't sure he could pretend as good as Mom. But only crying at night was easier than not crying at all.

He lifted his chin and nodded. "I can do it."

Pa's face changed. The wrinkles in his forehead disappeared, and he smiled, the way he used to smile, and Sid's chest puffed up like a superhero.

"Good. Now what kind of punishment do you think you deserve?" Pa rose and took Sid's hand.

Sid hung his head. Usually they took away a toy, or didn't read him a bedtime story. But he'd been terrible this time.

"No more superhero movies? Ever?" He forced the idea out and swallowed hard. "And peas for dinner every night?" Please not forever. "And help Nana clean up the mess?"

"Hmmm…" Pa led him toward the door.

Out the kitchen window, Sid saw the smoke from the fires. The big black clouds seemed farther away than earlier.

"That might be a bit harsh. Maybe no movies for a week. And definitely help with the mess. But I suspect Nana would be happy with a simple sorry."

Pa's hand rubbed the top of his head before he pushed him forward.

Nana turned. She didn't seem mad. She looked scared, as scared as he'd been until Pa found him.

"I'm sorry, Nana." The words rushed out, faster than

his mind formed them. He wanted to run over and hug her too, but his feet wouldn't move.

For a minute, he held his breath, until she crouched and held out her hand. His eyes widened. A shiny red apple winked at him, and on the counter behind her a whole bowl full of the round red balls glistened.

"Let's make some apple crisp together, shall we?" she said with a smile, before she wrapped him in a hug so tight, he thought the tears might squeeze out again. She wasn't Mom, but she loved him too, and maybe, just maybe, she'd talk to him about Mom.

Goody Twoshoes
by

Mark Love

It was a dark and stormy night. No, really, it was. Sleet slammed into the glass outside my office like frozen confetti from a victory parade in Times Square. But I had no reason to celebrate. Except maybe the warm company of my Old Grand-Dad. I guess whisky to sip could be considered cause for celebration.

There hadn't been a client through the doors in so long I was contemplating a career change. My last assignment had been a divorce job and the wife still hadn't coughed up my fee. My visitor's chair was coated in dust so thick, an archaeologist might refuse to take a seat. Maybe I could get my hack license and prowl the streets looking for fares. Or the monastery might be interested in a new recruit.

I was still feeling sorry for myself when a shadow filled the glass portion of my door and knuckles grazed the pane.

"Bar's open." There was no attempt to hide the booze or rise from my chair. Any visitors at this late hour would have to take me as I was.

The door swung open, hinges creaking eerily. My guest remained in the doorway, whether from uncertainty or for dramatic effect, I couldn't tell. Nor did I care.

"Mr. Case? Mr. Justin Case?" Her voice was roses and honey, with a hint of southern belle thrown in for good measure.

"That's what it says on the door, sweetheart." If I'd

been a smoker, it would have been my cue to light one up.

"I need your help, Mr. Case." She hovered in the entrance, like a thoroughbred waiting for the gate to open before the championship race.

"Come in and take a load off, doll." I switched the desk lamp on high and tilted my fedora back. My shoulder holster needed adjusting, but I ignored it, not wanting to spook her by drawing attention to my big gun.

She sashayed in close enough for the light to reach her. She wore a man's felt hat, maybe a Stetson, and a tan raincoat that reached her ankles. She paused long enough to shake the moisture from the coat and hang it on the brass rack by the door. When she reached my visitor's chair, she nonchalantly flipped the Stetson behind her. It bounced off the door and settled on the hook. Smooth.

"What seems to be your problem, Miss…?"

"Twoshoes. Call me Goody."

I dumped the last two fingers of yesterday's coffee from my ceramic mug and poured her a jolt of the whisky. Alcohol sterilizes everything, right? "Have a blast, Goody, and tell me why you need my help."

She downed the shot like a sailor on leave. While Goody was avoiding my eyes and summoning the nerve to talk, I did a quick inventory. Auburn hair dangled below her shoulders, with just enough curl to get lost in. Green eyes chiseled out of an emerald perched above an aquiline nose that had never been wiped on anything short of Victorian lace. Soft, pouty lips painted in hot pink. A slender throat begged to be smothered in kisses. The body was shapely, concealed in a black wool dress that hugged her curves like a Jaguar on a racetrack. The legs were long and supple, wrapped in black silk stockings. Black stiletto heels covered her dainty feet.

"I think someone's trying to kill me, Mr. Case," Goody said in a throaty whisper.

"Just call me Case. What gives you that idea?"

"There have been three accidents lately. At least, that's what the police are calling them." She drained the last of the Old Grand-Dad into her mug and tossed it back without so much as a gulp. My throat burned just watching her.

"Tell me about the accidents."

"The first one was Monday. Then Tuesday. The last one was today."

I picked up my best ballpoint pen, the one from Al's Repossessions and Bail Bonds, drew a pad out of the desk drawer and rephrased the question. "What type of accidents?"

"Oh. Well, first the mirror fell on my bed. Then my cat died on the stairs. And today, it was poor Francis."

"I don't think the first two are much to get excited about, doll."

Goody ran the tip of her tongue across those hot pink lips and looked longingly at the empty whisky bottle. "The mirror killed Felix. Felix Flingeasy."

I paused in my attempts to determine if she was wearing underwear and studied her face. "The billionaire?"

"Uh huh. He was my uncle. Felix stopped by Monday to take me out to dinner. I'd been shopping all day and was running late. He came in and flopped on the bed while I was freshening up."

My mind whirled, trying to remember the details from Tuesday's paper about the city's favorite gigolo. Flamboyant Felix Flingeasy founded his fortune in furs, furniture and freighters. He supposedly had more romantic liaisons than Valentino and Casanova put together. Goody needed a little prompting. "And the mirror—"

"Had been mounted on the ceiling over the bed. It was there for months, a gift from Grandpa Twoshoes. Grandpa always said it was the best way to start the day, looking upon a sweet face like mine. The mirror crashed down on top of poor Felix."

"I thought the police determined he died during a domestic dispute?"

Goody sighed and shifted in her chair. She crossed her gams and then spent a few seconds smoothing her skirt around her knees. My mind, always alert, swung back to the underwear controversy. "Parts of the mirror shattered and cut him pretty badly. The police thought it was better for his image to play up the domestic problem."

"Tell me about the cat." My money was on a black lace bra with a thong and matching garter belt to complete her mourning ensemble. Of course, those could be thigh high stockings, so garters would be unnecessary. Or maybe a camisole.

"Fluffy died Tuesday. She fell down the stairs and landed on my fencing foil. She was never very graceful."

"You always leave your fencing foil lying around?"

Goody shook her head once. "I had a lesson Tuesday morning. Right after making the arrangements for Felix's funeral. Fluffy fell off her futon on the landing and was filleted by the foil."

"Fluffy had a futon?"

"Fluffy was Felix's favorite feline, Case. He felt a futon was appropriate for a frisky female like Fluffy. It was Felix's idea that I take fencing lessons, for safety's sake."

"Felix feared for your safety?"

Goody Twoshoes rose and began to pace the room. I noticed the dusty imprint my chair had left on her taut backside. Whether she was stalling or debating a point of information didn't matter to me. I was too busy enjoying the view. Goody paused by the window and studied nature's arctic blast.

"Felix seemed certain someone was trying to censor his activities. He sensed they might use my relationship with Felix to silence him."

I rocked back in my chair and propped my wing tips on the edge of the desk. "So far what you've described sounds like two accidents, Goody. What makes you believe someone's after you?"

"Francis was the final clue. He was fried to death." Goody blew a long sigh against my window and watched her breath fog the glass.

"Explain fried to death. And who was Francis?"

Goody drew a little design on the glass window before turning a profile in my direction. "Francis was a fish, Mr. Case. He was very rare. A priceless freshwater puffer-fish. Felix gave him to me for my fifteenth birthday."

"How was Francis fried?"

"In hot Wesson oil with a few flecks of fennel."

"Why would anyone fry your fish?"

Goody turned around and knocked my feet off the desk, then parked a dangerous curve on the edge. "Someone's trying to upset me. If they can succeed, who knows what I might do? You've got to help me, Case."

It was an effort to drag my eyes from her figure and

listen to what she was saying. Or what she wasn't saying. "Who stands to gain the most from your situation, sweetheart?"

She thought about it, drumming her polished pink nails on a supple thigh. There's something distracting about a woman in black stockings. "Wanda. She's the only one who could possibly be involved."

"Who's Wanda?" My notes were beginning to look like the membership to a secret club. Felix, flattened by the falling mirror. Fluffy, fallen from her futon and foiled. Francis, French fried with just a hint of fennel. I hadn't seen that many F's on one sheet since my high school algebra class. I turned the page and waited.

"Wanda Wildchilde. She's a distant relation to Felix, on his stepmother's brother's side of the family." Goody picked up my drinking glass—the one I'd swiped from the Hilton—and drained the last few drops of my whisky. She left a pink smudge of lipstick on the edge. I would never wash that glass. Not that I ever bothered to before.

"Are there any other relatives Felix might have? Someone else who might figure in his will or claims to his estate?"

Goody sighed. "No. There was no one else in his life. Felix favored flings, not wanting to be tied to any one person. He feared anything beyond a brief dalliance would drive a lover's motive toward greed. Felix showed me his will once. Other than a small amount he would leave Wanda, the bulk of his fortune would belong to me. We are his only remaining relatives."

"Was Wanda aware of the will?"

"I don't know."

"Only one thing to do, doll." I pushed back my chair and stood. "Let's go talk to Wanda."

Goody bounced off the desk. "Now?"

"Sooner we find out who's behind these accidents, the sooner you can relax and start spending your inheritance."

****

Wanda Wildchilde lived in Whispering Willows, a subdivision just west of the city, named for the enormous trees that guarded each house. Despite the late hour and the wicked weather, lights were shining from her windows as we parked at the curb. Goody was barely visible, tucked inside her coat and hat. We moved up the walk, ducking beneath wet willow limbs toward the entrance. There was movement behind the picture window, and I could see a roaring fire in the hearth of the brightly lit room. Goody clung to my arm, putting her trust in my prowess as a detective.

The door opened at my knock and Wanda Wildchilde waved us inside. We stood in the hall, dripping puddles on the woolen rug, while Wanda wished us well and welcomed us. I wondered what was going on.

Wanda could have been Goody's twin. Her auburn hair was wound up in a braid that nestled at the back of her head. But her other features, build, and mannerisms were exactly the same as Goody's. Wanda was wearing a baby blue lounging robe with white trim and worn leather moccasins. The question of underwear resurfaced in my mind. I'm a stickler for details.

"So where did you find the shamus?" Wanda asked Goody in a warm, sultry voice.

Goody moved into the sitting room and removed a cigarette from an ornate wooden box. She lit it and blew a plume of uninhaled smoke toward the ceiling. "What's the difference? He's willing to work on the accidents. The truth will come out."

Wanda fixed me with a withering stare. "Will it now? I'm willing to bet you don't know half of the story."

"What do you mean?"

Wanda moved to a sideboard and poured us each a snifter of brandy. My taste buds weren't accustomed to such riches, but I never turned down free hooch. "I'll bet Goody didn't tell you about the missing will."

"No, she forgot that part."

Goody flicked her cigarette toward the fire and missed. She made no attempt to retrieve it. Was I the only one who saw the carpet beginning to smolder?

"I didn't forget," Goody said. "I just didn't get that far. Case only asked who else would prosper from Felix's untimely departure. Naturally, I thought of you."

Wanda flashed a wicked grin. "Perhaps I should explain everything, Mr. Lace."

"Case. Justin Case. Explain away."

Wanda wandered over to a wicker chair with a thick pillow and wilted into the cushions. "It seems that Felix was more than a little cautious about his fortunes. After his funeral today, his attorneys informed us to meet at his home for a reading of the will. What we saw was not what we expected."

"What Wanda is trying to say in such a wayward manner," Goody interrupted, "is that Felix left us a puzzle to solve."

I had been staring at my snifter, wondering if it was polite to ask for seconds on brandy. "A puzzle?"

"Felix left a videotape for our viewing. Apparently, he felt his life was in danger recently. Felix feared for his own safety." Wanda wiggled to the sideboard and back and refilled my brandy. "So he left us the tape and hid the original will, after having his lawyer deliver the extra copies so he could add a codicil."

The brandy buzzed in my brain, and I could only nod at the beaming beauties before me. "So what's the puzzle?"

Neither one spoke. Instead, they came to stand before me, one on either side. The lights in the room and the glow of the fire answered the underwear question about Wanda for me, but Goody remained a mystery.

"Let's go to the study," Wanda suggested.

"An excellent idea."

Turns out the house didn't belong to Wanda. It was Felix Flingeasy's place. Rather than flaunt his wealth and seclude himself from the public, Felix liked to mix with the neighbors and be treated like a regular guy. Apparently he conducted many of his liaisons in the study, which was decorated like a men's club, with leather chairs, a billiard table, entertainment center, shelves lined with books, a bar and another fireplace. This one was cold, but it burst to life at the touch of the button under Goody's thumb, a reaction I could easily relate to.

Wanda wagged her head toward the leather chairs. "Play the tape, Goody."

"It's all cued up. Hit the switch."

We sat around a poker table, facing the television screen. With an auburn-haired lovely on either arm, I was beginning to feel like a playboy. Whatever Flingeasy had to say, I was ready to sit right there and listen, half a dozen times if necessary. The screen flickered once and then the image I'd seen in the paper appeared. He was well preserved for his age, with a full head of silver hair and a face as smooth as a baby's butt. Dark green eyes stared intently into the camera as the deep voice spoke.

"If you are watching this tape, then I must be dead. I can't believe either of you would ever harm me, but I've taken a few precautions. Just in case. All you have to do is find the will. You've got seventy-two hours and then it all goes to charities, particularly the Kennel Club and the Audubon Society. The proper combination can lead to the will. Be kind to each other. Work together and you can have it all."

The screen turned to snow and the women turned to me. Unfortunately, all of my finely tuned skills were currently focused on the lack of food in my system. Drinking always makes me hungry. What I wouldn't have given right then for a corn dog and some pork rinds.

"Well, what do you think, Case?" Wanda batted her lashes at me.

"Is there a safe in the house?"

Goody squeezed my arm. "Felix wouldn't stand for a conventional safe. He had to be different, extraordinary. If there's one in the house, it's in this room. But we can't find it."

"Check everything. There could be a hidden switch or lever that would reveal the safe's hiding place. Let's get busy." I struggled out of my chair and away from the women.

My vision was blurry. I made it across the room to the books and began to run my fingers over the spines. Wanda picked up on my idea. She yanked the volumes from the shelves, looking for a false panel or a safe hidden inside. No such luck. Goody had taken to the floor on her hands and knees, crawling under the table and checking the bottoms of the chairs for secret compartments. We searched the cupboards, behind the bar, inside the stereo speakers, the light fixtures, behind paintings, under the carpet and behind the dartboard. Nothing.

Outside the rain continued, joined by the rumble of thunder and the occasional flash of lightning. It was still a dark and stormy night.

"It's got to be here!" Goody collapsed on the floor and drew her knees up to her chest.

"The old boy's probably having a laugh at our expense," Wanda muttered. "Even dead, Felix is fooling around, having a good time."

I leaned against the billiard table and glanced at the two women. Even after the long night of tireless searching, they both looked as fresh as glamour models. Idly, I lifted the cue ball from the table and rolled it across the felt. It wobbled away from my waiting hand and bumped the burgundy seven ball. A soft thud met my ears.

"Who plays pool?"

Goody didn't raise her head. "I'm not in the mood, Case."

"One guy playing games with us is enough," Wanda said. "Even if he is six feet under."

I picked up the cue and the seven balls and rolled them together in my hands. There were only two other balls on the table. The solid black eight ball and the white and yellow nine. I peeked at the antique webs on several of the pockets and saw the rest of the collection scattered across the table. Banging the cue ball lightly against the seven gave off a funny sound. I walked around the table to a rack on the wall where polished cue sticks stood at attention and fresh boxes of chalk were stored. There was also a rack with an assortment of other balls, the ones used for the game of snooker. I lifted one of these and tapped the cue ball against it. There was a solid click. I hit it again, just to be sure, and then replaced the snooker ball.

"Felix play a lot of pool?"

Wanda boosted herself up onto the bar, bare legs dangling from the robe in a most unlady-like fashion. My theory on underwear was proven once again. "He loved to play games. Felix thought it brought out the little boy in him."

I returned the balls to the table and then lifted a stick from the rack. Neither woman was watching as I lined up the shot. The seven was in the center of the table, on top of a felt marker. The eight was tight against the rail, where a diamond chip marked the spot for a bank shot. The nine ball hugged the same rail, only inches from the corner pocket. I blinked my blurry eyes a couple of times, then snapped off the shot. Seven-eight-nine combination. The click of billiard balls making contact reached my ears, along with the soft swish of the nine dropping into the webbing. Then a machine started from somewhere beneath the slate as it rolled up like a sardine can's lid. The seven, eight and cue ball dropped into a small basket beneath the felt covered slate.

"Oh my god!" Wanda bounded off the bar and stood beside me. Goody joined us in a heartbeat.

Under the slate was a storage area about four feet long and two feet wide. There were packets of cash, folders filled with papers on various corporate dealings, and one large manila envelope, marked in thick black pen WILL. The women dove for it. I crashed into a club chair.

"How did you know?" Goody asked when she brought me a fresh snifter of brandy.

"The combination shot was set up on the table. The seven ball wasn't regulation. It's metallic, with some kind of sensor inside. It doesn't make the same noise that two ivory balls do when they strike. The table must be rigged with a system that opens when the right combination is made. There's probably a sensor on the rail, as well as one in the pocket and the eight and nine balls. The other balls are standard ivory. They wouldn't work."

Wanda stood beside Goody and draped an arm around her shoulders. "We should have known. That corny joke was one of Felix's favorites."

"What joke?"

Goody smiled. "Why was six afraid of seven?"

"Beats me."

Both women answered in unison. "Because seven ate nine."

I groaned and took another sip. I could grow to like brandy. "Tell me something, Goody. What made you look me up? You seemed pretty confident that I'd find the will."

"Felix said you would know." She kicked off her heels and sat in the chair beside me, topping off my glass again.

"I never met your uncle."

Wanda went to the stereo system and fired up a track of English rock music. A strong male voice begged to be her father figure. Wanda stared at me with a confused look. "Felix wasn't our uncle. He was our father. We were given different names to avoid any embarrassment to his image. How could he be a free-wheeling playboy if the public knew he was raising his children?"

My brain was getting as wooly as my Aunt Tilda's mustache. "Uncle, father, whatever. I never met him."

"But he told us to get you. On the tape. When he mentions taking precautions." Goody leaned against me and helped guide my glass up for another sip.

"He didn't mean me." I shrugged and gulped the last of the booze. My tongue was growing Angora sweaters. "It was a coincidence. Justin Case. Just. In. Case. Happens all the time."

The women exchanged wide smiles. "Dumb luck," Goody said. I thought someone was calling her, but it was a new song starting on the stereo.

"What about Fluffy and Francis?" I asked. "Who killed them?" Suddenly the demise of her pets seemed very important.

Goody patted my cheek. "Damn cat drove me crazy. I'm allergic to animal fur. Felix thought it was hilarious, the heiress to a furrier's fortune, unable to get near the animals. We used it for fencing practice."

"What about Francis?" My eyes could no longer focus on the two beauties. I was floating away on brandy clouds.

"Why, Mr. Case. Don't you know puffer-fish are poisonous? There was just enough left after we fed it to Felix to puree it and slip some into your brandy."

My eyes lost the ability to focus, but my ears were still working. Amid the pounding bass drum and the roar of electric guitars came the same repeated phrase.

"Goody Two Shoes- Goody Two Shoes,
Don't drink, don't smoke, what do you do?
Don't drink, don't smoke, what do you do?
Must be something inside."

The Number
by

Barbara Bettis

Caroline never saw it coming.

The number on the phone bill hit her like a baseball bat to the solar plexus. How could she not remember it? It was nearly identical to her birthday—555-1975. Fifth month, fifth day, forty-four years ago. She'd joked with Jerry when it first appeared. But that had been months ago. Months.

Paper clenched in one hand, she paced to the desk and pulled out the accounts-paid folder. There it was: twice in April and before that, three times in March. Jerry had said the calls were to an insured whose house was damaged in the tornado. As an insurance adjuster, he made and received dozens of calls about claims when disasters swept through the Midwest. But the same caller—now, in July?

July Fourth. Caroline had been in Dallas that weekend, visiting their daughter Kathy and her newborn son. Jerry had been too busy to meet his first grandchild. He'd remained at home to draw up estimates from the current disaster, a flood south of Chicago.

Caroline usually didn't question unfamiliar numbers. While most business calls came in and were returned on Jerry's personal cell, an insured occasionally called the house phone. But something about seeing this number again sent bile into her throat. She rubbed her clenching stomach.

Sucking in a deep breath, she made her way to the coffee pot. As she sat at the kitchen table, sipping a cup with her usual two tablespoons of Dutch-chocolate creamer, she glanced at the clock. And gave a bitter laugh. Ten a.m. The world trembled, precisely at ten a.m., her usual morning break time.

This all had to be a mistake. A ridiculous misunderstanding. She'd misinterpreted a silly phone number. Jerry would laugh and say it was just like her. He'd tell her not to worry, perhaps go to the salon.

She had a haircut three days ago. He hadn't noticed.

The phone bill lay on the table and she pulled it around to study it once more.

The area code—from St. Louis, she thought. A suburb, perhaps.

Her hands trembled as she raised the cup to her mouth. A drop slipped from the edge onto her fresh white top. For once she didn't leap to her feet, dash off to change, and put the stain to soak.

Instead her mind worried at unfamiliar doubts like a kitten with a ribbon. There must be a logical explanation like always before when a number reappeared several times over months. Such was the insurance business, Jerry told her, again and again. Some claims took forever to settle.

By ten thirty a.m., the trembling stopped. By eleven a.m., rebellion clicked in. Caroline rose, rinsed the cup, placed it in the dishwasher, then walked to the living room. She took a deep breath, caught her bottom lip between her teeth, grabbed the phone, and punched in—1-555…. Three rings, four….

"Jerry, sweetie." The soft voice was bright and cheerful. "I thought you were working near St. Louis this week."

Caroline jerked the receiver from her ear and

fumbled it back into the cradle, her determination gone. How could the woman have known who called? Caller ID, of course. The name Jerry Moore would have appeared at the other end.

All right. No need to panic. There was a perfectly reasonable explanation. But the chills across her shoulders wouldn't listen.

A shrill ring startled her, and she jumped. Staring at the phone, she at last eased it silently to her ear.

"We were cut off, sweetie," came the same soft, bright voice.

Anger flushed through Caroline, steeling her jitters.

"Jerry? I was surprised to get your call. Are you coming over next week?"

"Sorry, Jerry's not here." Caroline's throat was tight, her words calm. "This is Mrs. Moore."

A chuckle drifted from the receiver. "Oh, Jerry's mother. He's told me so much about you. I didn't realize you were visiting."

"I'm not, *sweetie*. This is his wife."

Silence. Then, "Does he know you're in his house? He told me all about your divorce."

Caroline's heart thumped so loudly it beat out the ringing in her ears. By some miracle, her voice remained steady as she said, "He told you all about it, did he? Just what did he say?"

The woman's soft voice wavered. "He told me about the other man, how you left with no word and took all the money. But that doesn't matter to me. I know you don't care about him, but I do. I don't need the money."

Ha! She'd be the first woman Caroline had ever known who didn't need money.

Lips clenched, she struggled with what to say next.

What DID one say to a woman who was sleeping with one's husband? Let him wear his socks to bed or he'll come down with a cold? Don't use fabric softener on his underwear or he'll break out in a rash? Make sure there's plenty of whole milk in the fridge for his midnight snack runs?

Her attention focused again when the voice asked, "You're not going to make trouble for us, are you? I love him and he loves me."

"No," Caroline said at last. "I won't make trouble for you. What *is* your name?"

"I don't think you need to know." Miss You-Don't-Need-to-Know hung up.

Breathing through her mouth in steady draws, Caroline put the phone down and headed for the computer. The reverse phone lookup website found the name: CeCe Dixon owned 555-1965.

Never heard of her.

Caroline sat for a while, her mind numb. Finally, she looked around at her tasteful Colonial living room. The walls snapped beneath a new coat of spring-green paint. Every stick of Early American furniture saluted in its place. Not a speck of dust cowered on the antique oak floors. The usual gratification at such perfection eluded her.

She needed to think.

The clock showed it was eleven fifteen a.m. Only fifteen minutes for her trembling world to shatter. What should she do?

She'd clean the kitchen. Cleaning helped focus her thoughts. She always cleaned when she was upset. She always *cleaned...cleaned...cleaned*. The phrase echoed in her temples.

In the sparkling mint-and-stainless steel kitchen, she put on her plastic gloves and placed a bucket in the sink to fill. For once, she didn't worry about the new black-granite fixture. What did she care if it scratched?

How could this have happened! Surely there was some mistake. What could Jerry have been thinking? Now, wait. She was overreacting. Twenty-six years of harmony could never be disrupted like this. There must be some reasonable explanation.

The sound of water overflowing caught Caroline's attention. "Damn," she muttered, turning off the faucet. She winced. She never swore, not even the mild "chickie swearing" of her church group.

Perhaps one of her friends from the fitness club would have insight on the problem? No.

Maybe Liz was back from L.A. at last. Drying her hands—she didn't even notice she still wore the gloves until she'd finished—she dialed her best friend.

Liz wasn't home.

Caroline left a rambling message, then stood with the receiver in her hand.

Surely this person, this CeCe, was lying, was stalking Jerry. Her husband's sultry eyes and dimpled chin drew the stares of women like flies to a garbage pail. Over the years, women had made all sorts of excuses to call him about one claim or another—cars damaged in parking lots, roofs dinged by hail. The two of them had laughed many times over the persistence of desperate females.

This female hadn't sounded desperate. She'd sounded…nice. Surely not.

Still, how could Caroline know for sure?

Was there anything else that could tell her? Where

could she look? Jerry's company cell? The credit card bill? She always handled their house bills, but Jerry took care of the company's. Those records would be in his safe.

She made for the bedroom. His company safe was locked. Of course it would be. What was the code? She punched in every set of numbers she could think of—his birthday, their wedding anniversary, Kathy's birthday, his office phone. Nothing happened. Pausing, heart in her throat, praying it wouldn't work, she punched the last combination she could think of—555-1975. The door opened.

She removed a sheaf of papers and sat on the floor. Thirty minutes later, she knew. These weren't only bills and receipts from the company's card. They were also from Jerry's personal card—one she didn't know he had. And bank statements from an account she wasn't on.

For months—years—Jerry Moore, devoted husband, loving father, church pillar—had lied. To everyone. Even to himself, if he thought he would get away with it. Sweet CeCe, at the other end of 555-1975, was not the first.

Caroline found bills and receipts from jewelers and lingerie shops, even from an adult toy shop, some going back years. A few had names, phone numbers, descriptions written on them. And charges at hotels Jerry had always told her were much too dear for them to frequent on vacation.

Then, from the back of the safe, she pulled out a large manila envelope. She upended it into her lap. Money. Hundred dollar bills, a few fifties thrown in, all neatly divided into stacks of a thousand. Twenty thousand dollars. It hadn't come from their joint checking or savings accounts. From where, then? And why?

She shoved the envelope back, then meticulously replaced every sheet of paper and relocked the safe. Just as meticulously she blanked her thoughts. Deadly calm, she

straightened any disorder left in the room and walked to the living room.

Cold. What had happened to the temperature in the house? Caroline was freezing. She sat. And thought. And waited. For her high school sweetheart, for her soul mate, for her adulterous husband to walk through the door.

When he did, she was smiling. "Tell me about CeCe," she said. She could have laughed at the look on his face. She didn't.

A long time later, after tears and recriminations and promises of innocence, they sat together on the rust-and-green-plaid sofa. Jerry stroked her cheek.

"I would never be unfaithful to you," he said for the fourth time. "This woman has been hounding me for months, since the tornado hit. But I'll take care of it, I promise."

His charcoal-gray eyes smoldered with what he must imagine was devotion. They were bright and sincere. She didn't believe him for a moment. She'd seen the evidence. Even a note or two he'd been sentimental enough to keep.

"I just need a bit of time to recover from the upset of the call," she told him sanctimoniously. "I'll sleep in Kathy's room tonight. You understand, don't you?"

"I understand completely," he assured her. "I have some paperwork to finish anyway." He faced her before he left the room. "Why don't we get away next weekend?

Maybe a trip to Chicago?"

"To a hotel overlooking the lake?" she asked, recalling one of the receipts she'd just seen. "The penthouse suite?"

Jerry laughed and gave her a hug. "Sweetie, that's way beyond our budget.

Find us something else, why don't you?"

Caroline lay awake that night, staring at the midnight-blue ceiling which she had painstakingly spackled with silver stars when Kathy was five. Tears trickled from her eyes into her hair. How did one cope with the devastation of such a discovery?

He was lying. She knew it. She also knew he didn't realize she knew it. What steps should she take? Divorce, of course. But surely she could do something—one little thing that might make him realize the pain he'd caused her.

Clutching a pillow to her face to muffle the sounds, she sobbed.

The clock winked three ten a.m. as she finally sat up and clicked on the bedside lamp. Her tears had long since dried and she'd outlined a plan. Caroline clenched her teeth. Jerry Moore wanted to be a lying cheat? Fine.

Slipping out of bed, she pulled a very large blue duffel bag, nearly as tall as she was, from the back of Kathy's closet. It hadn't seen service since Kathy went to camp years ago, but it was perfect. She stuffed it with a few books wrapped in extra blankets and some of Kathy's old clothes, then knotted the ties and tugged it to the door. Smiling, she returned to bed. Later, she'd complete her plan.

The following morning, before the sun had time to stretch out, Caroline prepared Jerry's favorite bacon, egg, and cheese biscuits. When he got home, he promised, he'd make things right.

"Of course I believe you," she assured him, lovingly kissing his cheek.

He patted her back. "Tonight, everything will be so different, you'll wonder how you could ever have doubted me. No more separate bedrooms, huh?"

He pinched her bottom. He was in his best high-school-quarterback looks as he grabbed the keys and his briefcase.

"Later, sweetie."

Caroline smiled and nodded at their traditional farewell. "Oh, wait," she called at the last moment. "I need to get rid of some of Kathy's old things. I've packed them up. Would you please drop off her old duffel bag at the thrift shop on your way? You know I can't handle such heavy things."

She smiled her sweetest helpless smile as Jerry dragged the heavy bag out to the company pickup and heaved it, at last, into the bed. Through the window over the sink, she could see their neighbor Carl taking out the morning trash as usual.

He lifted a friendly wave to Jerry. He even offered to help with the very heavy bag.

Jerry, of course, refused.

Carl watched as Jerry drove off.

Carefully, Caroline donned the rubber gloves from yesterday, punched in 555-1975 on the safe's keyboard, and removed the twenty thousand dollars. She put her own breakfast dishes in the dishwasher, leaving Jerry's on the table.

The moment Carl and his wife left for work—both taught at the nearby high school—she picked up the manila envelope and her purse and walked to her sedan, waiting in the garage.

Eventually, the car would be found six hours away at the St. Louis airport. Eventually, police would discover the heavy blue bag Carl saw contained just what Jerry insisted. Eventually, she would telephone Kathy from Italy, the trip he'd insisted they couldn't afford for their twenty-fifth anniversary.

Eventually, Jerry's attorney would receive her divorce papers.

But not yet.

Not until Jerry understood the feel of a baseball bat to the belly.

Deadly Homecoming
by

Peggy Chambers

The Christmas lights pulsed in time with the artery pumping blood on the ground. Lying on the frosted ground, she saw the white lights in the distance grow closer, blinding her. Bridget shielded her face, trying to roll out of the way as the horn blew - she heard the air brakes slam.

"Ma'am? Ma'am? I'm gonna get you some help. Just stay still," the trucker said, dialing his phone. Then everything went black.

****

Eight months later

As the road stretched out before Paula, she glanced at the passenger next to her. Her daughter stirred, rolled her neck, and sat up.

"Where are we?" Bridget stretched and yawned.

"Just entered Kentucky." She smiled at her daughter. When she first woke up, how much she looked like the little girl Paula had raised.

Leaning over Paula's shoulder a wet nose snorted, and large blue eyes stared back at her from the rear-view mirror. They belonged to a chocolate-colored Labrador retriever. Wiley was a Christmas present from Bridget years ago when Paula didn't know she needed a dog.

Parking the car, she glanced at her damaged daughter. It had been eight months since the beating, and she was still fragile. "What do you say, you hungry?"

Bridget pushed her sunglasses up, shoving her short dark hair straight up on her head making it stick out like a fan. "Yeah, I am. And I'll bet Wiley needs out."

Only a few weeks ago, Bridget would hardly touch food - no matter what it was. The doctors told her mother it was a sign of depression and not to give up. The recent interest in eating again was a big step in the right direction. Paula didn't care if she ate soup lapping it with her tongue like a dog - as long as she ate.

****

The phone woke her from a deep sleep that awful Christmas night. The voice said her only child was in critical condition. Wiping the cobwebs away, Paula was certain it was a wrong number. Bridget couldn't possibly be lying in a hospital bed beaten beyond recognition. But there she was, a bloody purple lump that looked enough like her daughter to make Paula want to faint.

Over the next few months, Paula had taken a leave of absence from her teaching job and stayed home to help Bridget heal. But, the external pain was the easy part. It was the mental scars that held Bridget in a vise grip. Her depression came and went with the weather, and it was always cloudy in Seattle.

"Mom, you have a packet from an attorney's office," Bridget said bringing in the mail. At least she would go out to the mailbox. She wouldn't for a while. Slowly, Paula got her to go out to dinner and a few places.

Paula ripped open the packet thinking it must have something to do with her daughter's medical bills.

It wasn't. A legal letter attached to probate documents said her uncle in Kentucky – the one she had seen once in her life – had died. Being his only heir, she was left his hard-earned fortune, a horse farm. Paula tossed it aside. Surely there was a mistake.

But she soon learned it hadn't been a mistake. She was an heir to a farm in Kentucky. What would she do with a farm but sell it? And she had more important things to do than worry about a real estate sale right now.

After dinner that night, the idea came slowly at first, and Paula once more picked up the legal documents, looking them over. Kentucky had to be sunnier than Seattle. And a trip might be just what the doctor ordered. They needed a journey.

"Bridget, what do you think of a road trip?"

Her daughter shrugged as usual. Anything was okay with her as long as it didn't require too much effort. The decision was up to Paula.

A week later, they entered Collinsville. Google directions said her uncle's farm was a few miles east of town, but they needed a break and some information.

Paula pulled into the parking lot of a convenience store as a rusty old red pickup pulled up at the other end. A tall, thin man in dirty faded jeans climbed out. The women watched his long legs saunter up to the door and walk in, pulling the door shut behind him. His black – almost blue - hair shined in the afternoon sun.

At the counter, Paula spoke to the clerk. "Hi, I'm Paula Abernathy. My uncle used to have a horse farm around here. Ron Williams?"

Bridget stepped up beside her with two cherry colas.

The young woman behind the counter wiped down the counter with a rag. "Ron was your uncle?"

"Yes, and I wanted to see his farm. I understand it is east of here not too far. We're just in from Seattle."

"Seattle! Long ways away," said the girl as she rang up the drinks.

"Yes, it is. Can you give me directions?"

The loud crash sent all three women scrambling.

"Luke? You okay?" The girl behind the counter leaned over to get a better look. "Is the display in the way?"

"No, sorry, Meg. My fault. I need to watch where I'm walking," The man from the pickup leaned over and righted the display of chips.

"Sorry, ma'am. Luke's a little clumsy sometimes. Now if you take the highway here to the left and drive about five miles, it's the first house on the right. You can't miss it; big two-story house with a white fence and a long driveway." She handed back the change.

Paula thanked the clerk and headed back to the car.

Stopping the Jeep at the driveway that looked just as the girl had described, she saw the mailbox read *Williams*. "I guess this is it." Paula looked apprehensively at the house. They took the shady winding driveway slowly. Straddling the middle of the gravel and dirt lane, the tall grass brushed the underneath of the car.

"I'll bet this was beautiful once." Bridgett looked around at the house and pasture.

"Well, beautiful or not, it's ours." Paula opened the door of the car and let Wiley out. He stretched both ends, then shook – stiff from the long ride in the car - and searched for a tree.

Paula shaded her eyes looking up at peeling paint and torn screens. Then noticed the front door stood ajar.

"Oh, that's nice. I just assumed the place would be locked up. Doesn't it seem odd that the fences are recently painted and there are two horses over there, but the door is open?"

"I don't know, but we are about to have company."

Bridget nodded behind her mother.

Almost on cue, Wiley ran toward the horses barking wildly as the old red pickup pulled into the driveway blocking any exit.

"Hey, knock it off!" the man yelled as he climbed out of the truck. "Lady, that dog has no business scaring my horses. Call him off!"

"Wiley!" Paula called. "Wiley! Come!" She shouted, slapping her leg to get his attention. Wiley immediately stopped and ran to Paula's side.

"I'm sorry about Wiley. He's normally very well behaved. I'm Paula Abernathy and this is my daughter, Bridget."

The young man with the blue-black hair took off his sunglasses and baseball cap, running his hand through his sweaty hair. He eyed the women closely.

"You were in the store back in town," he said without introducing himself.

"Yes, and you ran over the new display of chips." Bridget attempted to appear taller. "What did you say your name was?"

"Luke Masterson, I live about a mile over." He pointed to the other side of the field. "I worked for Ron before he died. Since then, I've kept my horses here, and looked after the pasture."

"Well, Luke, it is nice to meet you." Paula sized up the young man, looking him up and down. "I inherited this place from my uncle. I've never been here before, and we made a road trip out to see it. It's obvious that the meadow has been looked after. Someone has even painted the fences recently. You?"

"Yes, ma'am, that was me. Having the horses here kept the tall weeds from taking over and gave them something to eat." He smiled at Bridget. She looked away.

"Do you know why the front door of the house is open?" Paula pointed to the porch.

"No ma'am. Let's take a look." He yanked the door open, and something scurried across the floor.

"You first." Paula gestured to Luke, shrinking back.

Bridget looked around. "Great Halloween spook house. Complete with spider webs."

Dust motes floated on air currents as they walked through the door.

"Yeah, it's been empty a while." Luke sounded non-committal.

"I guess I should apologize if I came on a little strong back there. It's just that I kind of think of this place as mine since I worked here so long, and I didn't know who you were. So, you ladies are going to take over the place?" Luke eyed Bridget. "It would be nice to have neighbors again."

Paula looked around at the dirty windows and floors. It hadn't been cleaned in a long time. "I don't know yet. I had a key and thought we might stay here while we got it on the market. But, under the circumstances – where's the closest Holiday Inn?"

Luke again snuck a look at Bridget. "Not into nature, huh?"

"Not this much nature."

"Well, there's a hotel up on the highway, down from the convenience store." Luke pointed in the direction of town.

Wiley ambled over and looked up at the stranger. The young man rubbed the big dog's ears. Paula trusted Wiley's instincts about people.

****

The man with the scarred lip looked through binoculars at the farmhouse - his green sedan hidden by the trees. It had been a long drive since he left the attorney in a pool of blood. He never intended for his ex to leave Seattle, but her bitch-of-a-mother got in the way. But this might just work out after all. They were in the middle of nowhere and no one knew them. Now he could get rid of them both.

****

After a good night's sleep in the Holiday Inn, Paula and Bridget drove back to the farm. Stepping up to the porch Paula froze in her tracks. "We need to get a locksmith out here today. The door is open again."

Luke appeared in the doorway, sticking his head out the door.

"Morning ladies." Luke smiled. He was much cleaner than yesterday. Even the porch looked swept.

"Luke, didn't we lock up before we left last night?"

He stood with the sun reflecting off his hair. "I don't think it latches and your uncle really didn't believe in deadbolts. I hope you don't mind, I tried to tidy up a bit. I really felt badly about the way I acted yesterday. I guess I've been out here by myself too long. So, to show you that I'm really a good guy, I did a little cleaning up. And the mouse we saw is gone."

Bridget shuddered. They stepped in the door of the large living room. The windows were open, and a breeze blew across the hardwood floors. Everything had been swept and dusted.

Paula stared around the room. "Did you work all night?"

Luke nodded. "I don't sleep much – so I decided to

put my insomnia to work. It could be cleaner with some soap and water, but the utilities aren't on."

"That's very kind of you. Have you had breakfast?" Paula indicated the box of pastries in her hand.

Bridget carried the coffees and handed one to Luke. They sat on the porch in the morning sun eating rolls from the deli and drinking lukewarm coffee like old friends. Maybe Luke wasn't so bad after all.

Luke put his phone back in his jeans pocket and took a bite of the cinnamon roll. "I called my friend at the City and he'll send someone out to turn on the water. They require a deposit, so you'll have to go back into town to pay that. I think I can get the other utilities turned on too."

****

The clerk stamped the receipt "Paid" and slid it across the counter to Paula.

"So, you're Mr. Williams' niece?" The clerk nodded to Paula.

"That's right." Paula placed the receipt in her purse.

"I'm glad someone's living in the farmhouse. Welcome to the community."

Bridget was looking out the window but turned and spoke. "Thanks, but we won't be staying. We're putting the place on the market."

"Well, there was a man in here yesterday looking for a place – I don't know if he wanted to buy or rent – but he mentioned the farmhouse. A nice young man – I didn't get his name – he said he was looking for the Williams' place. I directed him out to your farm. I hope that was okay." The clerk looked at Bridget's startled face.

"What did he look like?" Bridget asked.

The clerk stammered, "Well, he was nicely dressed in blue jeans and a button-down shirt, brown hair and no hat - and I remember he had a scar on his lip like he'd cut himself."

Bridget bolted for the door.

"I didn't mean to get in your business. Can I do something to help?" the clerk said quickly.

Paula cleared her throat. "Yes, tell me where to find the sheriff." The clerk pointed next door. "And if he comes back, call me at this number." Paula slid a card across the counter and then ran for the door.

In the Jeep, Paula opened the glove box and took out the handgun that was always loaded, stuffing it in her bag. Wiley scooted closer to Bridget.

"We have a room at the hotel, the realtor is meeting us at two o'clock and she knows someone to do the cleaning. We can be out of here and on the road in a couple of days – maybe less."

Bridget stared straight ahead. "How did he find us?"

"I don't know, but I am calling the attorney who sent us the paperwork." She rolled through the contacts in her phone.

"Mr. Haines, please. This is Paula Abernathy. Well, when do you expect him? This is an emergency." There was silence from Paula. She glanced at Bridget. "When did this happen? Thank you and I'm sorry for your loss," Paula said into the phone and clicked off.

"What's wrong?" Bridget wrapped one arm around Wiley.

Paula's next words were the last thing she wanted to say to her shattered daughter. "Haines was murdered in his office a few nights ago."

****

The sheriff sat on the porch swing taking notes. Bridget told her story again rubbing Wiley's ears as the locksmith worked on the doors. The details were always the same, but each time she told it, she became more concise. Paula hoped that was a good sign.

"So, the suspect, Dan Harvey. . ."

Bridget sat rigidly. "He isn't a suspect. He beat, raped, and left me for dead. If the trucker hadn't found me, I'd be dead now – and he probably just murdered our attorney."

"Well, I'm sorry ma'am, but in the eyes of the law he's innocent until proven guilty and he never went to trial. That makes him a suspect. I'm not sayin' I don't believe you. But for now, we have to call him a suspect. I'm going to call the Seattle police and have them send me the file. It might be a good idea for you to move into the hotel in town where you're easier to watch too."

"We have a room in town," Paula said.

"Good, and locks on the doors here at the house. Bobby there is the best locksmith in the county."

A pink Cadillac pulled down the driveway, blowing up a cloud of dust.

"Looks like you've got the best realtor in the county too." The sheriff nodded as a woman in suit and heels stepped out of the car, waving as she trotted up to the porch.

"Hi! Madeline Wichert, realtor. You called me?" She shaded her eyes and looked at the people on the porch. "Sheriff, I hope there's no trouble already." The realtor's pearly white teeth shone in the sun.

Paula rose and walked toward the steps. "I'm Paula Abernathy. I called. We'd like to put the place on the market at soon as possible. We're in a bit of a hurry."

"Of course. Let me get my contracts." She reached back in for her briefcase in the car.

"I could stay here tonight if you would like." Luke rocked back and forth in the outdoor chair. "Like I said, I don't sleep much and having someone at the house, might be a deterrent."

Paula shook her head. "No, Luke, you've done enough, really. We'll be at the motel and the house will be locked."

The sheriff stood. "I don't think it's a bad idea. If someone is in the house, it's less likely that a break-in will occur."

"Well, if you really don't mind." Paula glanced at Luke and he nodded.

****

Sheriff Monsees' cruiser was backed into the trees. With a good view of the house and Luke on the inside, he felt like things were secure. The horses would alert him if anyone came from the back.

The late summer air blew through the window. It was almost Labor Day. The stores would soon have the Halloween decorations out. His grandkids were back in school. That meant the holidays were right around the corner. His wife was already planning the Labor Day celebration. It was always a big deal at the Monsees' home.

His radio crackled. "Sheriff," said a breathless Deputy Sam Smith.

"Go ahead," the sheriff replied. Smith was always rattled about something. He wondered what it could be this time.

"The hotel in town is on fire. We got everyone out and I'm headed your way with the women."

"On fire! What happened?"

"Sally thinks it was an explosion."

The radio crackled again. "Good Lord in heaven! Bring them out here pronto! Over and out." He grabbed his cell phone to update Luke.

****

Paula was holding her emotionally broken daughter as she sobbed.

The sheriff stood beside them. "Did you actually see him?"

"We didn't see anything. We heard the explosion and then the deputy banged on the door. But we're sure it was Dan Harvey. Wiley growled at the door earlier."

"The dog knows his scent?"

"Yes, he knows him."

Lifting her head and staring at the sheriff with red rimmed eyes, Bridget spoke in a quaking voice. "Sheriff, I was married to Dan for two years. Two of the worst years of my life. I know him, Wiley knows him, and so does my mom. We know it was him."

The sheriff nodded. "Okay now, Deputy Smith, Luke, and I are going to stay here with you. I know it won't be easy but try to get some rest." He pointed to the mattress on the floor.

"Tea?" Paula asked nodding to Bridget who nodded back. "Anyone else?"

Paula found a tea kettle in the messy kitchen. She always had chamomile tea bags in her giant purse. It had a soothing effect on Bridget. Taking mugs from the cabinet, she placed a tea bag in each one when she saw movement out the window.

"Sheriff!" she shouted. "There's someone out back!"

The deputy headed for the front door. Paula snatched her purse off the chair fumbling for the gun as Luke pulled her into the living room.

Sheriff Monsees eased the door open with this gun drawn, shining the flashlight in an arc across the backyard when Wiley flew past, a deep growl in his throat. Running out the door, all the sheriff could see was a pile of arms and legs on the ground with a growling, snapping dog on top of them. Screams of pain and terror emanated from the dark pile. "Get him off!" screamed the man on the ground. But Wiley had one arm in his mouth and was not letting go.

"Mrs. Abernathy!" the sheriff yelled. Paula came running down the back steps.

"Wiley off!" She commanded with shaky authority. The dog stopped shaking his prey and looked up at her. He still held the limp arm in his mouth. "Sheriff, this is your suspect, Dan Harvey."

The man with the scar on his face looked up. "Paula, get this mutt off me."

"Wiley," she said quietly. "Would you like to have this man for dinner?"

****

Paula woke to the smell of coffee brewing and a knock on the front door. The realtor in her always-sparkling Cadillac stood at the door with an armload of breakfast rolls and an army of people. The workers were unloading equipment. There were ladders ready to assault the dirty windows and painters in stained white uniforms with rags hanging from their pockets. The marines had landed.

Bridget stirred, stretching as she sat up. "Do I smell coffee?" she asked.

"Yes, Luke made it." Paula opened the door to survey the crew. "And we have company."

Within days the farmhouse looked like new again. Fresh paint, clean windows, and polished floors. But the best part of the transformation was the one that took place in Bridget's smile.

The realtor sign in the front lawn was soon taken down. Bridget decided they should stay at least through Labor Day since the sheriff asked them to come to his annual bash. And she had assured Luke that he would love her grandmother's chess pie recipe.

****

The day of the party, the house was so crowded that when the sheriff's cell phone rang he had to step outside to hear. Luke sat with Bridget on his lap eating their pie.

Monsees spoke into the phone. "Harvey, escaped?" The sheriff looked up at Bridget.

Her plate shattered as it hit the ground and the smile disappeared from her face.

Monsees looked up from the pile of pie and broken plate. "Bridget, where's your mom?"

"Mom went back home," she said quietly.

****

Wiley had been the hit of the party. He managed to beg scraps from almost everyone. When Paula ran home to get more whipped cream, she took him with her to be sure he didn't eat anymore.

Taking her overly large purse up the steps, she rummaged for her keys as Wiley emptied his too full belly in the grass.

The front door swung open as she reached for it with the key. Rough hands dragged Paula in the house, the screen door slamming shut. Paula was thrown to the floor holding tightly to her purse and the gun. Coming up off the floor quickly, she held the gun in both hands and pulled the hammer back.

Dan smiled.

"Go ahead; you don't have it in you."

As she squeezed the trigger, Dan lunged low, hitting her in the stomach. The bullet flew over his head. Wiley burst through the screen door as Paula's head hit the floor and the gun flew from her hand.

The big dog was on top of Dan in an instant but, stretching, Dan reached out for Paula's gun. Grabbing it, he fired. Wiley went down with a thud.

When Paula woke, the room swam before her eyes. She could see Wiley in the corner panting heavily.

****

"Stay here, Bridget!" Luke said, kissing her quickly and running for the sheriff's car. "I'll be back as quick as I can."

"No!" Bridget called as the sheriff's car blew down the road.

She wouldn't be left behind. She surveyed the yard finding the pink Caddy was nearest the exit and Madeline's purse closest to the door. She'd bring it back, but she'd borrow the car – even if she had to steal it.

****

The sheriff handed the shotgun to Luke. "That will take out a lot more than birds. Circle around the back and keep your head down. I'm going in the front." He trotted up to the torn screen door and took a deep breath.

Sheriff Monsees burst through the front door unannounced, finding Paula tied to the chair, eyes wide with fear. There was something dark in the corner. And then the lights went out and the sheriff dropped to the floor. Dan stepped out from behind the wooden door with a baseball bat in his hand. The sheriff's blood decorated the end of it.

As Luke rounded the back of the house, he found the deputy at the base of the steps in a puddle of his own blood, but still breathing. Suddenly, the wind was knocked out of Luke as the bullet hit his shoulder, slamming him to the ground. The last thing he remembered was seeing Dan's face over him as he passed out in pain.

Dan leaned the shotgun against the table and looked at Paula. She was awake. He knocked her chair over and dragged her out the door where the deputy and Luke lay in the back yard, then went back for the sheriff.

****

Sneaking up to the house, Bridget quietly made her way inside. There was blood on the floor and Wiley lay in the corner. Snatching up the shotgun, she racked the slide and tip-toed quietly toward the noises in the backyard. Dan stood over her mother, holding a gun to her head.

"Call her!" he shouted. "Call her now!" Paula sobbed, holding the phone and shaking her head.

Cold fury stole through the younger woman as she breathed deeply - reveling in the feeling. Calmly, Bridget felt an inner strength she never knew she had. "No need to call her, I'm right here."

Dan whirled around, gun in hand, but Bridget fired first.

Dan Harvey fell with a dozen pea-sized holes in his chest seeping blood on to the ground.

****

The fire crackled beside Bridget and Luke sitting by

the Christmas tree, Wiley at their feet. Her new diamond ring sparkled in the firelight - she spun it around on her finger. The scent of turkey wafted through the air as Paula worked busily in the kitchen making their first Christmas dinner in the new house. The presents were opened, but the best present was the smile on her beautiful daughter's face.

"Merry Christmas baby," Luke said kissing Bridget's tiny baby bump and handing her a Christmas ornament - a beautiful child in a manger for the new baby.

An Egg-Cellent Witness
by

Marilyn Barr

I just had to stop for coffee on the way to the courthouse and celebrate my first big win as a scientist. I'm not old enough to drink, but my discoveries are making a difference. My data is going to take down one of the biggest polluters in the midwestern USA, and I get to be an expert witness for my state's environmental protection agency (EPA). That's why I had to grab a giant chocolate mocha with whipped cream and chocolate drizzle. I babbled to the barista about my expert scientist status and received extra whipped cream without the upcharge. I got a mountain of topping precluding the lid from sealing correctly and now I'm coated in chocolate mocha.

No problem. I'm a college student who visits my parents only to do laundry and half my wardrobe hangs in the back window of my car. My only white dress shirt is chocolate frosted, so I don a white V-neck under my navy suit. I still made it into the courtroom before they called everyone to rise for the judge and with the bottom half of my coffee intact.

The jury shuffles into the courtroom like a plague of zombies. Long-bored faces, without a smile among them, gaze over the crowd until they lock their vision on the attorneys. Each juror's face turns into a sneer as if daring the attorneys to drag this out any longer. I have been waiting over a week for my turn to testify, and the jury isn't convinced by the prosecution's case.

Experts from the EPA who did follow up studies based on my data prattle on about the mysterious gram-negative rod-shaped bacteria. We cannot name it without conjecture or basement level statistical area of confidence. As each day ends, I get more and more nervous. If we were allowed to make the leap from serotype number to bacteria's common name, the jurors would decide guilt in a snap. Hopefully, a snap after they hear me speak. I made the initial discovery; shouldn't I have gone first?

"I would like to call Ms. Amy Jensen to the stand," calls the prosecutor. *Finally*. I jump out of my seat like a game show contestant. Hop, step step. Excitement coils in my legs and they want to skip to the front of the room. Steady, steady. I must look dignified. Regal, yet approachable. Knowledgeable, but not a know-it-all. Hop. Steady, step, step.

The bailiff gestures to the witness stand, and I sit down with a creak. The aging leather chair is cracked with daggers of pleather aimed to attack anyone with normal width thighs. It sags to the left due to a broken spring. I compensate by leaning to the right. I don't even get to put my hand on a Bible, but raise my right hand for swearing to tell the truth. I place my mocha on the graffiti-covered ledge at the front of the box only to have it picked up by the bailiff. He casually drops it in a neighboring trash can with a crash that could be heard three states away. RIP Mocha.

"Ms. Jensen, will you please tell the jury the motivation behind your involvement in the investigation against the Thomas Egg Farm?"

Huh, what? I'm ready to talk about my detective work. I'm prepared with my data. I have spreadsheets. I kick myself mentally for not pressing the attorney for a prepared question list, but I thought my data said it all. Feelings and motivations aren't my strong suit. "I got a cold sore and—"

"Objection! Witness has no medical training and cannot self-diagnose," yells the defense attorney. I shoot him my meanest glare. The glare I reserve for punk freshmen who think they can steal the mini-glassware as souvenirs from the class I assist. The attorney is not intimidated by me. No surprise. I bet he played rugby on scholarship and goes by Butch, Brutus, or Buddy on the weekends. The fist he bangs on the table to punctuate each word is the size of my head. Brutus, it is. Brutus is my nemesis.

"You should say you felt a sore spot in your mouth," the judge says, turning to me. The kind notes to his voice are reflected in his lined expression. I repeat his words verbatim and get a nod of approval. Good girl.

"What was your next course of action when you found the sore?"

Here's where it gets dicey. Do I tell them about the fight I had with my boyfriend over the cause of the sore? We carried on for hours over whether or not he kissed anyone else the previous weekend. I found pictures on his fraternity's social media page where he was the main attraction. He was drunk as a skunk, but not dressed like one. He wasn't dressed at all. Nope, not going there.

"I came to the conclusion I must have an infection from the bad tasting water at the science fair where I was a judge," I say proudly.

"Objection! Witness has no medical training and cannot come to such conclusions without data," bellows Brutus. He reminds me of my little brothers who interrupt until you forget what you are saying. I feel my temperature rise and dampness collect beneath my jacket. He will not pull me off-track.

"I will get to the data when I get to that part of my story. I have spreadsheets," I snap. Oh, that was bad. Brutus smiles like a grinch while sliding into his chair. The prosecutor shoots proverbial daggers at me from the beads behind his spectacles. Even the kind expression of the judge is melting. I chance a glance at the jury who is sympathetic to my plight. They want me to get to the good part as fast as the attorneys will allow me.

"I'm sorry," I mumble.

"The events discussed lead you to collect data from the location of the science fair," says the prosecutor looking at the judge for approval. The two exchange nods over my head like I'm a child who is awake past her bedtime and acting out. "Where was the science fair?"

"Riverside Middle School. It was the twenty-seventh annual—" I stop when the prosecutor puts his hand up to stop me. I guess he has decided we will be communicating primarily by gestures.

"How did you test the water?"

"I collected the water from all the women's bathroom sinks and water fountains in sterile vials to take back to my university's lab. There I inoculated blood agar plates with the water using a crosshatch streak for isolation and gram-stained to identify the colonies," I say. Getting to the scientific jargon puts me at ease. In the lab, I'm a beast, and they are going to hear my roar.

"What did you find from the initial tests?"

"I found gram-negative colonies of rod-shaped bacteria." My sweet demeanor was returning.

"What did you do with this data?"

"I started writing my paper," I blurt out before I have a chance to think. They didn't mean literally, moron. I could have skipped to the next sciency part. As it is I left it wide open for—

"Objection!" Of course, Brutus objects. He's like a super-sized doll with a string on the back. Pull the string and he says, "objection, objection, objection." Several members of the jury roll their eyes.

"Your Honor, we are discussing the assessment of thousands of dollars in damages to my client not to mention the loss of revenue due to the public exposure of this case. I move to dismiss. The initial inquiry is based on her science homework," he sneers. Brutus waves an arm at a rotund man in a shiny cowboy hat, seated in the front row. The man leans onto a rhinestone-crusted cane to the point he is practically at the defense table. Rings glitter from his every finger, casting colored photons on the ceiling. Could the cowboy be Mr. Thomas?

"Your Honor, that's a bit melodramatic," pleads the prosecutor. His whining focuses me on the matter at hand. I must be careful not to be hypnotized by the cowboy's rings again.

"My dear, was this data originally for a class?" The judge leans over the partition between us to glower at me. I take a moment to formulate my answer. I look at the jury to find several small smiles, which fuel my bravado.

"Yes and no," I say proudly. I was mistaken when I thought the judge was glowering before. His previous countenance was an unkind expression. I'm definitely getting a glower now. "I collected the data for my senior project, but I'm not yet a senior. I wanted to get the data before the homecoming festivities, the holidays, the snowy months, and my senior activities with my sorority." My planning and responsible nature shocked the entire courtroom. Every face wears an identical mask of shock and awe. It is rare someone of my age plans in advance; I let my pride show.

"Your Honor, my client's livelihood and the livelihood of the hundreds who work for them are put in jeopardy around the schedule of homecoming activities," Brutus says in a voice strangely close to my own tone. First, he tries serial interruption, and now- he's imitating me. I would be a let down to annoyed big sisters everywhere if I let him get the best of me.

"I will end the testimony of this witness when I see fit," declares the judge. I fight the urge to stick out my tongue at Brutus. "Now, my dear, did you show this data to your advisor or a member of the faculty at the university?"

"Oh yes," I gush. "Dr. Andrews was very impressed. He said it—"

"Stop, stop. You can't tell me what he said. Stick to yes or no, okay?"

"Okay," I say with vigorous nods. Brutus is the one acting like a child, but somehow, I'm on thin ice. I haven't been able to show them my spreadsheets yet.

"What was the next thing you did to investigate?"

I sit quietly. How can I answer? I fidget in my seat causing it to groan obscenely. The prosecutor leans on the front ledge of the witness box. When he lifts his arm to wave at me, I notice some of the graffiti has transferred to his sleeve. Being labeled "Stinky McNumbnuts" fits him like a glove.

"I collected more water samples from the watershed around the school and drainage ditches to look for the same type of colonies."

"Did you find them?"

"Yes, I told my advisor, and Dr. Andrews said…sorry. I collected water samples from further away but still following the same watershed to the river. The ones east of the initial samples had the gram-negative rod-shaped bacteria, but the samples to the north and south did not."

"I would like to enter Exhibit A into evidence," says the prosecutor. My heart jumps into my mouth. Here is my moment.

Exhibit A is a map of my county with the cutest pink icons representing the gram-negative, rod-shaped bacteria. The pink icons are the exact same shade as the gram-negative stain. The samples without the potentially pathogenic bacteria were given a lonely black icon. The result is a pink-frosted trail of cookie crumbs linking the farm to the school. I beam with pride while the map is projected onto a screen over my head. I gaze at each juror for a reaction. They are sitting at attention, fascinated by my masterpiece.

"Please continue with your procedure." The tone of the judge's command pops my soap bubble dream of wowing the courtroom. I better keep moving before Brutus decides to object again.

"I obtained permission to isolate the DNA of the bacteria and serotype it from my advisor. I had done the procedure many times in class and—" I got the hand from Beady Eyes…again.

"Please BRIEFLY describe the method for serotyping," the judge says with a wince.

He needn't be worried for I have the directions memorized. We had to know it backward and forward for the pre-lab quizzes in Dr. Andrew's class. I talk through each step being diligent to name every piece of equipment and solution I used in excess of the kit while relating the finer points to the PCR machine. I would have added the history of the method, but I got the hand…again.

"Okay, okay, no more. I would like to enter exhibit B into evidence," he says. He takes off his glasses and rubs his eyes. Poor attorney. He must have strained his beady eyes shooting daggers at me.

I squeak with excitement when my serotype spreadsheet with map overlay is projected above my head. I get glares from both attorneys at my outburst, but I'm too distracted to care. The map is a three-layer opus of statistics, equally appreciated by the jury and myself. The bottom layer is the watershed with water flow direction indicated in blue. The second layer is the strain identification number in red. My only regret is the serotyping machine doesn't spit out the bacteria's common name in big red letters, only a strain number. The final black layer is the probability the sample matches the identified strain. Our school colors are blue, red, and black. Go Bears!

"Can you briefly, I mean with less than five-hundred words, describe exhibit B?"

I describe my masterpiece with a flourish. I count my words on my fingers and use the graffiti letters as placeholders for batches of hundreds. I've reached my choice of design colors when I'm out of words.

"No further questions," says the prosecutor. I do a happy dance in my seat until it groans again. I hope no one thinks the noise is coming from my body. I sit up straight, and the chair nearly capsizes due to the lean. Oh well, bon voyage chair. I'm outta here.

"The defense can cross-examine the witness," says the judge. What? I look at Brutus. He is leering at me like he's taking measurements for my coffin. A bead of sweat drips from my hairline down my spine. I swallow the nerve-induced sawdust caught in my throat and wish I still had my mocha.

"Are you nervous today, Ms. Jensen?"

"Not until now," I reply drily before I can censor myself. I hear the twinkle of laughter flow from the jury box.

"Well, I am very fair. No need to be nervous. We only want the truth right?"

"Riiiiigggghhhht."

"Did you collect all the water samples yourself?"

My pulse thunders in my ears. How could he know? The only ones who know are my boyfriend and me. Remembering my oath, I give a defeated, "No."

"No?" Brutus makes an exaggerated face and places a hand over his mouth. He looks like a circus clown who is about to pull a fast one on the tough guy. My pals on the jury aren't buying his act. They are shooting daggers at him for taunting me.

"No," I say with more ire. I take a centering breath to hold my temper within my lungs.

"Please tell the jury which samples were obtained by you and which data is not yours," he says with an evil grin.

"Only Sample #11," I say with my most confident voice, "was obtained by Jeremy Larken, my boyfriend."

"Your boyfriend?"

"Yes, there was a spider."

"A spider? Hundreds of jobs on the line—"

"It was a really large spider with a yellow symbol on the abdomen." I get answered by another ripple of giggles, but this one travels around the room.

"Which is more important the spider or—"

"Objection! Counsel is asking for the witness to state opinions outside her area of expertise," bellows Beady Eyes who has found his second wind. The judge nods, and I give a smirk to Brutus.

"Withdrawn," Brutus replies with a wave of his hand. "Do you eat eggs, Ms. Jensen?"

"Oh yes," I reply. "I'm on a keto diet. It requires a large quantity of protein and good fats like the ones found in egg whites—" I stop when Brutus gives me the hand.

"Do you buy Thomas's eggs when you grocery shop?"

"No, I—"

"No further questions," Brutus says. He santers back to the defense table and pulls on his jacket lapels as he sits. Cowboy uses his cane to roll Brutus's chair into the audience's front row. Holding him hostage with the cane across his chest, Cowboy begins to berate Brutus with terse whispers. Brutus goes from smug, to thoughtful, to sheet-white.

"Prosecution would like to have a rebuttal with this witness," says Beady Eyes in an obsequious tone.

"Make it quick," barks the judge. It must be close to lunch for him to be cranky.

"Ms. Jensen, is there a reason why you do not purchase Thomas's eggs?"

"Yes, I'm a college student and eat all my meals in

a cafeteria. I do not grocery shop unless it is for feminine hygiene products." I can't believe my ears. My embarrassing response will be immortalized in the witness testimony for all time. A roar of laughter echoes throughout the courtroom and the judge bangs his gavel repeatedly. I'm excused and exit the chair with a loud squeak. Shuffling to the audience, I get a smile from Beady Eyes.

"The Prosecution rests," says the smiley attorney. I bite my tongue to keep from sticking it out at Brutus.

"So does the defense," Brutus declares. A collective gasp fills the courtroom. Et tu, Brute?

I guess everyone was fed up with this case because as soon as the prosecutor finished his closing argument, which was brilliant in my opinion, the defense asked to meet with the judge in chambers. Whatever Cowboy said to Brutus, it has given him a case of laryngitis.

The jury is ecstatic and practically runs to their sequestering room. Not only do they get lunch, but it is already set up and waiting for them. My stomach growls loudly and I wonder how much dignity I would lose if I went after my mocha in the trash can. If it stayed upright, then the contents would be unspoiled, right? I'm starving and my special treat cost as must as I make in a three-hour class teaching freshman chemistry lab.

When the judge and attorneys return to the courtroom, events pass by in a blur. The defense has decided to settle. The judge's chambers held a mediation where Cowboy agreed to pay an outrageous fine to the state EPA for the watershed clean up. My maps convinced him to settle. I feel it in my bones. My data is a bubblegum pink arrow pointing directly at his chicken coops. Coops leaking chicken poop. A breeding ground for salmonella: a gram-negative, rod-shaped, pathogenic bacteria known for causing intestinal distress, projectile vomiting, and in small doses, cold sores.

I walk out of the courtroom with the prosecution while they high-five and hug each other. They don't dare include me in the celebration. I'm the expert scientist in this drama and a step above their team. Reporters swarm us and Beady Eyes handles the questions like a pro. I remember my senior picture coaching and focus on keeping my chin down and head angled while the photographers get their front page shot.

Amidst the hubbub, Cowboy leads Brutus out of the building by his jacket lapel. I follow the pair to their awaiting limo. Cowboy climbs in while still swearing at everyone and everything. As Brutus leans into the car, I tap his shoulder.

"No hard feelings," I said offering my hand in a truce.

He gives my offering an icy glare as if I am the one dripping salmonella over the countryside. "Feelings? Little girl, I am a professional. My feelings weren't in the courtroom. When you grow up, you will see the difference."

I retract my hand and cross my ankles sheepishly. My toe twirls a few inches off the ground. "You are right. I'm not a grown-up like you. Have a nice life," I say sweetly as he sits in the car. I push his door closed but not before snagging the bottom hem of his jacket with my toe. The action gently blouses the blazer bottom close enough to me to trap within the car door. As the limo speeds away, I wave goodbye to Brutus's jacket flapping against the dirty asphalt.

Checkmate.

Season of Withered Corn
by

Judy Ann Davis

It would later be known as the Season of Withered Corn. But White Feather, for years to come, would remember it as a time of rejoicing, despite the fact that the Great Spirits had turned the land into the face of a wrinkled old woman and made the leaves on the trees grow sad and limp.

On a ledge in the hills overlooking their camp, he had lingered one afternoon, silently watching as the sun singed the grass in the valley the color of deer hide. Underneath the haze settling in, he could still make out his brother's wife, Morning Star, carefully carrying her birch bark vessels from the river to feed the thirsty beans and cornstalks, already shriveled, their wilted leaves turning yellow. He knew she would also carry water for his family's corn, now that his own wife, Little Sparrow, was about to give birth to their fourth child.

Just outside the birthing lodge, his three sons listlessly played a game of stick ball in the scorching heat. He knew they were not pleased when he had ordered them to remain in the village and forbidden them to swim or play near the river. But the lack of rains had forced the snakes and wild animals to seek shelter in the cattails and brush along the water's edge, and even the bobcats were leaving the forest in daylight to hunt the areas at the rim of the village.

White Feather had come to the rocky hills to be alone—to think. Before darkness fell, he knew he would have to choose a suitable name for his fourth son, yet the spirits had not given him a sign for many moons. It must be a dishonor, he thought, to have a child born during such unfavorable times, when even the berries in the forest had dried and fallen from their stems.

In the distant, thunder rumbled, and White Feather cursed aloud. For weeks upon weeks, the fickle spirits had played games with them, banging on their sky drums and tricking them into believing the clouds would shed some tears on the parched land.

Last night, when he had voiced his fears his son would be born during a barren time, Little Sparrow had only smiled, rubbing her swollen, extended stomach. "What if it's a girl?" she had asked.

But White Feather knew better. He was from a family of five brothers, and the gods had only seen fit to give them all sons. Besides, he had carefully watched Little Sparrow carry this child. It could only be a strong brave the way it kicked, somersaulted, and rolled restlessly inside her, so that many nights she was unable to sleep.

Rising from the ledge, White Feather moved toward the small footpath that wound its way down to the village. Thunder rumbled again, and the sky grew dark as ominous black clouds rolled in, blotting out the sun's scorching rays. A wind from the north lifted and sifted the leaves on the maples, and flashes of lightning sliced the horizon in two.

Minutes later, before White Feather was able to reach the flat land of the valley, the rains began, sweeping in with a roar like a buffalo stampede as they pounded the hard-packed earth and brittle thickets. Leaning into the wind, he trudged forward, despite the blinding wall of water that stung his face, drenched his breechcloth, and filled his moccasins.

In the village, White Feather found his people gathered outside their lodges. Laughing, chanting, oblivious to the pelting rain soaking the ponies and dousing the cooking fires, they celebrated and shook their turtle shell rattles and gave thanks to the gracious gods of rain.

Morning Star, chilled and wet to the bone, greeted him as he slogged through a dirty puddle. "The baby has arrived," she said, smiling and waving him toward his lodge, "and they are both well."

White Feather nodded, pushed back the flap to the entrance, and ducked inside. The smell of damp wood ash from the dead fires drifted in, mingling with the hot stagnant air of the sealed lodge. On a mound of buffalo robes, Little Sparrow lay holding a howling bundle in her arms. Her tired, sweat-streaked face smiled as White Feather shook the rain from his hair, and her eyes darted to the side of the lodge where the rain drummed a melody on the bark sheets between the gentle rolls of thunder.

"There is your sign," Little Sparrow said, softly.

White Feather grinned and moved closer to get a peek at the chubby red face wailing louder than the winds of winter. "It is good," he said. "We will call him Black Thunder."

Little Sparrow laughed, her voice rippling like the trill of a songbird on the morning breeze. She pushed herself into an upright position. "No, we will call her Singing Rain," she said, holding the noisy bundle out to him so he could see for himself the truth in her words.

Beneath the Pines
by

Debby Grahl

Hilton Head Island, South Carolina, 1911

Lightning flashed as the tall sea pines surrounding the old two-story plantation house swayed wildly in the rising wind. Ancient live oaks groaned and cracked as the sky darkened and the rain fell. Thomas Shelton stepped from the house onto the wide porch and peered into the darkness. Blinded by the sheets of rain, he heaved the burlap and oilskin bundle over his shoulder and, raising his lantern, hunching into the wind, made his way through the sodden grass until he reached a thicket of trees.

Here, somewhat protected from the rain, he found the tree he was looking for and deposited his burden at its base. As he reached for the shovel he'd placed there earlier to mark the spot, a gust of wind almost knocked him off his feet. Around him branches snapped. He held onto the trunk of the tree for balance, praying he hadn't waited too long. In his forty years on the island he'd lived through a few hurricanes, but something told him that whatever was coming now was going to be horrific. But he'd had no choice. He needed to wait until it was safe. The treasure had been in his family for nearly one-hundred fifty years, and there were those around him he didn't trust.

Earlier he'd sent his few servants to the mainland and planned on rowing himself across the sound when he was done. As he began to dig, the wind died down, and the rain stopped. Other than the water dripping from the trees, everything around him went silent. Unease prickled the back of his neck as he shoveled out more of the sandy soil. Just a little farther down and he'd be finished. A twig snapped behind him, and he whirled around, shovel held high. Surprise filled his eyes as his visitor entered the circle of lantern light.

"Good evening, Thomas."

Thomas peered into the darkness hoping his visitor was alone. "What are you doing here?"

The intruder smiled. "What do you think? I've come for what is rightfully mine."

"I have nothing that belongs to you, sir."

"I beg to differ. If I'm not mistaken, what you are in the process of burying—" He tapped the sack with the toe of his boot. "—was stolen from my family, and I've come to reclaim it."

"We stole nothing from you. Samuel acquired these riches honestly. If your ancestors were careless enough to lose them, it is not my fault."

The intruder's face darkened with rage. "My ancestors were upright merchantmen. Yours were nothing but pirates and thieves. With the storm coming, I knew you'd either take it with you or bury it, so I've been watching."

Thomas kicked the sack into the hole. "Then, sir, you've been watching in vain." He lifted the shovel high. "For I will never relinquish my riches," he yelled over the roar of the rising wind. Torrents of blowing rain whipped their faces, and a mighty gust unbalanced both men. Thomas swung the shovel at the intruder's head, who ducked and lunged, slamming into Thomas, sending both men to the ground as a mighty crack sounded.

Hilton Head Island, October, 2016

Tears of relief filled Emily Hope's eyes as her VW bug rounded the curve, and the house came into view. Even after the worst hurricane to hit the island in a century, the old plantation house still stood. As she had waited out the storm at her cousin Darla's in North Carolina, the reports had been sketchy. All she knew was that there had been structural damage, and thousands of trees were down.

She parked as close to the house as she could and stepped from the car. Petite, with chin-length blond hair and big brown eyes, Emily assessed the damage. Huge live oaks and tall sea pines lay tangled like giant pick-up sticks, but none seemed to have landed on the house. Cautiously she stepped over fallen branches and piles of debris, slowly making her way toward the back of the house. As she rounded the corner, her heart sank. She hadn't been as lucky as she'd thought. A huge pine tree had crushed the roof of her screened porch. Emily sighed. Considering the destruction she'd seen driving across the island, only having a tree on her porch wasn't so bad. The rest of the property was another matter. How would she ever clear out all the fallen trees? Again sighing, she headed for her car. She'd unpack then begin looking up contractors.

As she crossed the wide front porch and unlocked the double oak doors with their beveled glass inlays, love for the house washed over her. When she'd first found the house three years ago, she'd known it was a place she could call home. Built in the 1850s, it was in need of some repair, but it seemed to call to her. Two stories with a four-columned porch, tall windows with wooden shutters, and a sweeping crushed oyster shell drive epitomized the Old South. Emily pictured ladies in hooped dresses fanning themselves while sipping mint juleps, horse- drawn carriages coming up the drive, and handsome men in broadcloth and straw hats sitting upon their horses. Always fascinated by images of the antebellum South, she'd quickly applied when she'd come across the job opening to head the Beaufort County Historical Museum.

She'd been born in Boston, and her father was the owner of a fishing charter. One of Emily's first memories was the smell of the sea and the rocking of the boat. Her mother had loved to sail, and they'd taken their twenty-eight-foot sailboat up and down the coast. When Emily was away at college, her parents were caught in a storm, their bodies never found. Devastated, but knowing her parents would want her to finish her education, she obtained a degree in history.

An only child, she'd sold the house in Boston and the fishing boat. Then, just before her twenty-fifth birthday, she'd accepted the museum offer.

Emily carried her bags up the carpeted curving staircase to her bedroom. To Emily's delight, the previous owners offered to leave most of the antique furniture. A carved four-poster bed with a hand-stitched country quilt dominated the room. A matching cherry wood dresser, chest of drawers, and vanity completed the decor.

Emily unpacked and headed to the downstairs study she used as an office. Thankful the power was back on, she placed her laptop upon the roll-top desk and began to search for contractors. As she scrolled down the list, her doorbell rang. Frowning, wondering who it could be, she rose and headed for the door.

The man who stood on the porch took her breath away. Over six feet, he was lean but muscular. His hair was a rich dark brown and his eyes a smoky gray. Emily had to swallow before she could say, "Hello, can I help you?"

When he smiled, she thought she'd melt right there in the doorway, *For God's sake get a grip,* she told herself. *You've been alone too long.* Her friend Patty had wanted to introduce her to a guy she knew at work, but since her break-up with her previous boyfriend, Emily wasn't interested in dating. If she was going to react like this whenever a good-looking man showed up at her door, perhaps she should reconsider.

"Hi, I'm sorry to bother you, but I saw your car and thought I'd stop by. I'm Josh Campbell. I live up the road a ways. I see you have a number of trees down, and I wanted to know if you'd like help removing them?"

His southern drawl rolled off his tongue like silk, and Emily had to concentrate before she could reply. "Um, sure. Actually, I was just looking up contractors. Do you have a tree removal business?"

He smiled and nodded. "My family does landscaping." He stepped back so she could see the logo on his truck. "I can help you with the debris. I can also cut up some of the trees to make it easier to remove them."

Emily finally had her wits about her and smiled

back. "Mr. Campbell, please come in. You sound like an answer to a prayer."

As he walked past her, Emily couldn't help but notice how nicely his jeans fit.

"Would you like a soda or a beer?" she asked as she led him into the kitchen.

"A beer sounds good." He glanced around. "What a great house. How long have you lived here?"

"Three years."

"Do you know the history?"

"A little. I did some research at the Heritage Library. It was a small Sea Island cotton plantation, but a few years after the Civil War, the owners went broke. It was purchased by a family named Shelton." Emily shivered and rubbed her arms. "I discovered that during the 1911 hurricane, it's believed the owner drowned trying to row to the mainland, and the property was sold. It's a little weird that I'm living here during another hurricane."

"Yes, but you're safe and sound."

Emily smiled. "You're right. So how long have you lived on the island?"

"Just a year. My dad retired and wanted me to take over this part of the business."

"Where did you live before?"

"Beaufort. That's where I grew up. I decided I didn't want to make the commute, so my brother took over that half of the business, and I moved here."

"Well, if you can help me get rid of this mess, I'm glad you're here. Should we get down to business? How much is this going to cost?"

Josh laughed. "Don't look so grim. It's not as bad as you think. And I have a confession to make. I've seen you a couple of times but hadn't had the nerve to ask you out. So, when I saw that I got back to the island before you, I walked around and assessed things."

For a minute Emily just stared. *Go out with him? Did she hear right? Could the hurricane have brought her the man of her dreams? Don't be a ninny. Go out with him.* "Ah, well, I'm not sure what to say," she stuttered.

He smiled. "Say you'll have dinner with me tonight."

Emily hesitated for only a moment. "Okay, sure."

Josh's smile widened. "Great. Here's the estimate for the tree removal." He slid a piece of paper across the counter. "See, it's not so bad."

The cost was very reasonable. She looked up at Josh and nodded. "You're hired."

"Great. If it's all right, my brother and I will be here first thing in the morning. Since the hurricane, he's been helping me out."

"No problem. I'm an early riser." She sighed. "Now all I have to do is find someone to repair the back porch."

Josh grinned. "Actually…"

Emily rolled her eyes. "Don't tell me, you're also a carpenter."

****

Emily awoke the next morning to the sound of chain saws. Recalling her dinner with Josh, she smiled. Only a few restaurants had reopened, and they'd gone to Local Pie for pizza. She hadn't enjoyed herself so much in quite a while. *I'll invite him here to dinner tonight.* The museum was still closed, so she didn't have to go to work. She got out of bed and headed for the shower.

Because everything in the fridge had spoiled due to the power outage, she'd go to the Piggly Wiggly and stock up.

A short time later, as she headed for her car, she noticed in the distance Josh standing in an area thick with fallen trees. Puzzled as to why he was working there, when trees closer to the house needed to be removed, she shrugged and started her car.

****

Later that evening, they sat in the kitchen alcove next to a large window overlooking the yard.

"This was a delicious dinner," Josh said, laying down his knife. "I might be from the Lowcountry, but there's nothing better than a good steak."

"Thanks. I'm glad you enjoyed it. I thought that since the house survived the storm, we should celebrate," Emily replied.

Josh took her hand. "The storm also brought us together."

Emily's cheeks reddened. "Yes. Um, can you stay for a while? We could sit out on the porch swing."

He nodded. "I'd love to."

The scent of the marsh and the sound of crickets and frogs filled the night. Emily sat next to Josh and he cleared his throat.

"There's no easy way to ask this, so I'll just ask. Do you have a boyfriend?"

Emily ducked her head to hide her smile. "Um, no, not at the moment."

Relief filled his voice when he continued. "Great. I really enjoyed myself tonight, and I'd like to see you again."

Emily glanced up into his handsome face, his eyes lit by the glow of the living room window. "I'd like that."

"There's something else I'd enjoy doing."

"What's that?"

"Kiss you."

****

A couple of hours later, unable to sleep, her lips still tingling from Josh's heart-stopping kisses, Emily sat in her den going through the stack of mail that had been delivered that day. A wide grin spread across her face when she opened the envelope from the ancestry site she'd sent her information to. Following along her family tree, she was surprised to see Hilton Head Island listed. Her eyes opened wide in disbelief. According to the document, her ancestor, Samuel Shelton, lived in the area in the 1800s, and Thomas Shelton lived on the island in the early part of the twentieth century.

She shook her head in amazement. *Could I actually be living in the house of an ancestor who drowned during a hurricane? That would be way too weird.* She knitted her brows in thought. Her maternal grandmother's maiden name was Shelton, and all of Mother's people loved the sea. Again she shook her head. No wonder she was drawn to the house at first sight.

She glanced at the clock. Midnight. She'd lost all track of time. Yawning, she placed the genealogy in her desk, turned off the light, and headed upstairs.

Her mind jumping from Josh's kisses to the revelations about the Sheltons, Emily couldn't sleep. The light from the full moon streaked across her bedroom floor. A faint scraping sound from outside made her sit up in bed. It sounded as if someone was digging. Puzzled, she went to her open window and listened. Yes, it was definitely digging.

She bit her lower lip. *Should I call the police? But what if it's just a night creature making the noise? I'll just go take a look myself.* She rolled her eyes. How many movies had she watched where some stupid female hears something in the basement and goes to investigate?

She cocked her head. Now she discerned men's voices. She frowned. *It sounds like Josh. But what would he be doing out there this late?* Curiosity getting the better of her, she threw on jeans and a warm sweatshirt and headed down the stairs.

Emily quietly went out the front door and made her way around back. The brightness of the moon helped her see, but also made her too visible. She ducked down behind some magnolias and strained to hear. It sounded like they were arguing, but she couldn't quite understand the words. She crept closer.

"Damn it, Jeremy, this isn't right. We should tell Emily."

"Why? This belongs to our family. She has no claim to it."

"It's on her land," Josh replied. "Besides, who knows if that story is even true."

"Marcus Campbell died trying to get this back. It's been hidden for all these years. If it wasn't for the hurricane and the trees coming down, we would never have found it."

Unable to restrain her curiosity, Emily stepped from the bushes. "And what exactly have you two found?"

Josh, his face grim, stepped toward her. "Emily, please go back to the house. I'll explain later."

Emily brushed past his outstretched hand and gasped. There, at her feet, laying in a pool of lantern light, was a human skeleton. "What in the world?" was all she could say.

"Emily, please come back to the house," Josh pleaded.

She narrowed her eyes and pointed to the other man. "Who is this guy, and what's going on?"

Josh sighed. "This is my brother Jeremy, and these bones, if we're not mistaken—" He indicated the skeleton. "—are Mr. Thomas Shelton."

Speechless, Emily stared from one man to the other.

"You might as well tell her," Jeremy said. "Then we can get on with it."

Giving his brother a sour look, Josh turned to Emily. "Supposedly a man named Samuel Shelton stole a fortune in gold coins from my ancestor. During the 1911 hurricane, Marcus Campbell confronted Thomas Shelton as he was burying the coins. The men struggled, and Thomas was crushed beneath a falling tree. Marcus, caught by the same tree, had his right arm and side severely injured. He made it home but only lived for a few days. Delirious with pain, he rambled on about coins buried beneath a tree on the Shelton land." Josh shrugged. "Before the hurricane this property was thick with trees and no one knew where to look."

Incredulous, Emily gaped at the skeleton, then turned back to Josh. "You're telling me gold coins are buried here? How did you ever find this spot?"

"When the live oak toppled over, its roots revealed the skeleton," Jeremy replied.

"You see, we kind of, um, scouted out your property before you got back on the island," Josh said.

"Yeah, and if you'd stayed away one more day, we'd have had the gold, and no one would have known."

Emily placed her hands on her hips. "Well, I'm here, and I'm calling the police. Gold or not, this was a human being, and the remains need to be collected and buried. In fact, I just found out tonight that I'm related to the

Sheltons, so that makes me responsible for him."

Josh opened his mouth to speak, but Jeremy spoke first. "I don't care who you're related to. I'm taking the gold."

"We don't even know if the coins are here," Josh said.

"Whether they're here or not, I'm calling the police," Emily said.

"Emily, please, can we talk about this?" Josh asked.

Heartbroken over Josh's betrayal, Emily turned and ran toward the house.

The force of the blow to her back sent Emily to her knees. Gasping for breath, she tried to rise. Then her head exploded in pain and blackness. As she lay semiconscious, blood trickling down her face, she heard Josh shouting.

"Jeremy, what the hell is wrong with you? You might have killed her."

"I don't give a damn. I'm not leaving without the coins."

"The hell you aren't."

Emily made out scuffling sounds, then a sickening whack, then silence.

The next thing she knew, she was lifted and thrown onto someone's shoulder.

"Josh," she was able to mumble.

"No, your boyfriend won't be helping you." Jeremy sniggered.

Her head pounding and her stomach reeling, Emily forced herself to speak. "Where are you taking me?"

She heard him chuckle. "I saw a big gator in the pond on the edge of your property. I'll bet he'd like a midnight snack."

Panic shot through Emily. She tried to speak again but couldn't form the words. Jeremy tossed her to the ground. Water seeped into her clothes, and the smell of the marsh mud filled her nostrils.

"Don't worry. I'll make sure you're dead before I throw you in. You'll never know what happens."

Absolute terror revived her enough to plead. "No, please, don't. You can have the coins."

"It's too late. You know too much."

A scream lodged in her throat as he loomed over her. Then he fell sideways, landing half in and half out of the pond.

"Emily, are you all right?"

"Josh," she whispered.

He knelt beside her. "I'm so sorry. I had no idea he'd become so deranged."

Moonlight illuminated his blood-streaked face. "Josh, you're bleeding."

"He knocked me out, but my head is thicker than he thought. Here, let me help you up." As his arms went around her, they heard ripples in the water. Turning, horrified, they watched as Jeremy's body was dragged into the dark pond.

"Jeremy!" Josh yelled, as he lunged for his brother.

Unable to speak, Emily stared as the alligator began to drag Jeremy under, Josh holding onto Jeremy's legs. When Josh's head went under, Emily screamed and stumbled to the edge of the pond.

Bile churned in Emily's stomach when Josh rose holding only his brother's shoe.

His face ashen, Josh slowly made his way onto the bank and dropped to the ground. "I tried to save him," he sobbed, tears flowing down his cheeks.

Emily, sick with horror, wrapped her arms around him. "I know. Come away. We have to call the police."

"I'm so sorry for putting you through this. Jeremy has been obsessed with the coins since he was a kid. And now look what it's brought him. How will I ever tell my parents?"

Her body trembling, Emily tugged at Josh's arm. "Please get up. We need to go into the house."

When he stood, his eyes held such pain Emily's heart broke. She held him tight and kissed him gently. "I'm here. Together we'll get through this."

"Considering all that's happened, I thought you'd never want to see me again."

Emily gave him a nervous smile. "I have to say, a hurricane, a skeleton, and a treasure in gold aren't exactly the usual way to begin a relationship, but I know I want you in my life."

"Are you sure?"

Emily nodded. "I know in my heart we are meant to be together."

He kissed her tenderly, placed his arm around her shoulder, and without looking back they walked toward the house.

Christopher Reisner
by

Linda Griffin

The thing you have to remember about Christopher Reisner's life is that he was perfectly satisfied with it exactly as it was. I don't mean he was resigned to never being happy; he actually was happy. He didn't care whether his life was not what other people wanted—it was what he wanted. He had always been something of a loner, absorbed in his own interests. He was a talented composer, a solitary pursuit. He loved chess but preferred to play online, without the distractions of personal interaction. He loved pure mathematics, which nobody he knew cared about, and he could study it entirely alone. He didn't really like to be with people. He supposed he should but found it awkward. He did teach piano, enough to make ends meet, but he had no investment in his students' lives, and no desire to increase or improve his classes. He had no ambition, no desire for glory or recognition. If a piece of music pleased him, that was enough. Nobody else had to like it or even hear it. He was content.

He was aware that the other members of his family were—how shall we say it?—more useful, more socially acceptable. His father was a veteran police officer, his mother taught French and drama, his sister Vanessa was a surgical resident, and his brother Patrick taught deaf children. His family loved him. They were proud of his talent and enjoyed his company, even though he never knew what to say to them. He knew everybody liked Patrick best, and he didn't mind. He liked Patrick best too. His parents' marriage was warm and loving, and they had always been each other's best friend, so he had not acquired the idea that relationships were hard work from them.

It was not true, as his college roommate had said, that he had no love life. There are all kinds of love. He had been in love for years with Amy Prescott. His parents and hers had been friends since college, and he and Amy had grown up almost like cousins. He was able to see her often, as a friend, and nobody knew about his deeper feelings for her. The adolescent passion he had first conceived for her had settled into something more comfortable. He was entirely satisfied to worship her from afar. He knew everything there was to know about her, including that she didn't feel the same way about him. Indeed, why would she? What did he have to offer? He didn't mind her going out with other guys, as long as they treated her well. He wanted her to be happy. She would make a wonderful mother, and he was not qualified to be the father of those children. He would care for her children because he cared for her and want to be in their lives, but like a favorite uncle, not a father. Children were messy and disruptive and required a lot of attention. They would interfere with his music and his studies and make demands on his time and his finances. He was certainly not emotionally equipped to love and guide them. Yes, let some other dude provide what Amy and her children would need, as long as he could continue to see and dream of her.

He was not upset when she announced her engagement. He was concerned, as any friend would be, about her choice, but everything he learned only confirmed his faith in her judgment. Keith had a good job and a sense of humor, treated Amy with respect and tenderness, and clearly adored her. Christopher developed a certain fellow feeling for him and was only a little envious when he reflected that Keith might come to know her better than he did.

He was of course invited to the wedding. The entire family attended—his parents, Patrick and his wife and children, Vanessa and her neurologist boyfriend, and Christopher, solitary as always. At Amy's request, he played the wedding march and the recessional in the church and her favorite song, "Happy Together," at the reception. A professional band had been hired for the dancing, though, and he had no excuse to sit it out. He dutifully did the fox trot with his mother and waltzed with the bride's younger sisters—she was the second of four girls. The youngest, Paige, was the one who introduced him to Elizabeth Grant.

She was Paige's roommate at UCLA, recently turned twenty-one and only in town for the summer. She was a slender, dark-haired beauty with a ready smile and more than her share of dance partners. He wasn't one of them. "You'll like Elizabeth," Paige said. "She's a music wonk, too."

Paige could be expected to say that sort of thing, and it didn't mean anything, but it gave him a place to start a conversation. "You're studying music?" he asked.

"No," Elizabeth said, smiling, her cheeks flushed with recent exertion. She smelled enticingly of vanilla and something more subtle. "She said that because she thinks there's something weird about playing the violin." Her voice was lovely, her tone matter-of-fact.

"You're a violinist?"

"No, I play—play *at* more like. It helps me think and

sometimes it helps me stop thinking. If you know what I mean."

Yes, he did. "But you're not studying music?" No, of course not, because she knew the study of music was impractical and useless, as everyone always told him.

"No," she said, almost regretfully. "I'm a math major."

"Really?" he said, surprised into confession. "I was a math minor."

She leaned confidingly across the table. "Paige thinks it's weird," she said, "but I love calculus. I'd rather do algebra problems than crossword puzzles any day."

He wondered if he could be dreaming or hallucinating. The punch *did* taste a little strange. Spiking it would be just like some of Keith's frat-boy friends.

He and Elizabeth talked for more than an hour. When one of the groomsmen asked her to dance, she declined. When the cake was cut, she waited until a young girl brought her a piece, gave it to Christopher, and waited for another one. She ate with gusto, licking icing off her fingers. She wasn't watching her figure or any such nonsense. When Amy was ready to toss the bouquet, Elizabeth reluctantly yielded to Paige's persuasion and joined the group of marriageable girls who gathered around the staircase.

Amy was a vision in her lacy white gown as she leaned over the stair railing, her face glowing with happiness. Christopher gazed at her with a kind of nostalgic pleasure, but as the bouquet arched through the air, he turned his gaze to Elizabeth. She was smiling, joining in the fun, but she didn't reach toward the bouquet. Vanessa caught it, and Elizabeth clapped along with the others. And then, without hesitation, she came directly back to his table and sat down. "Silly ritual, isn't it?" she said with cheerful indulgence. "So, what were we talking about before we were so rudely interrupted?"

He didn't know. He didn't particularly care. He was astounded to find himself, after so many years of single-hearted devotion to Amy, smitten with this enchanting creature, this calculus-loving violinist with her short curls and long eyelashes, her delicious laugh and sensible outlook. More astonishing still, she was apparently interested, intensely interested, in him. Of course he knew her focus on him wouldn't last. He might as well get it over with.

He introduced her to his brother. Patrick was his usual blond, charming self, holding one of his sticky-faced but adorable children on his knee. "Patrick is very nice," Elizabeth said, in a tone of stunning indifference. "What's your sister like?" Clearly something was wrong with this girl.

She was wonderful to talk to, though. He had never had a best friend, but he imagined this must be what such a relationship was like. It was as easy to tell her what he was thinking as it was for his parents to share their thoughts and feelings. He might even be able to tell her about the incredible thing that was happening to him.

"Have you ever felt," he asked, "when something happened, even something good, as if you didn't know who you were anymore?"

"Oh, all the time," Elizabeth said at once. "Even when I painted my bedroom."

"That's not exactly what I—"

"No, I mean it. I wasn't the girl with the blue

bedroom anymore. Scary."

Yes, she was right; that was what he'd had in mind, but bigger, scarier.

"I think I'm falling in love with you," he said, uncharacteristically reckless.

"God, I hope so," she said. "I'm not the girl who doesn't believe in love anymore."

It was the first of many wonderful conversations. He liked talking to her even more than he liked kissing her and he liked kissing her quite a lot. He also liked to watch her play the violin. She held the instrument tucked under her perfect little chin and smiled at him as she bowed. She wasn't great, but she wasn't at all hard to listen to. She asked him to play one of his own compositions for her, sat on the piano bench beside him, and leaned against his shoulder.

"Oh, my God," she said, when he stopped. "I am so not in your league!"

Perhaps not, musically, but she was very cute.

He taught her to play chess. She was a pretty good player but admitted she didn't like it very much. She would just as soon have him play online with strangers. "I'm too competitive to enjoy a game that can end in a draw," she said. Cute and honest. He really did love this girl.

Remarkably, Elizabeth loved him back, totally, selflessly, unquestioningly. For her love was easy, natural, blissful. It made her happy. It made her glow. It made her even more beautiful.

It made Christopher miserable. At first he thought it was because he wasn't used to sharing his life. He loved having her around, but he did regret his lost solitude. Although not so much, after all. She did understand when he needed his space, and he missed her when she wasn't around.

At the heart of his misery, he supposed, was the idea that if he could simply let go and be happy with her, he would have to admit he wasn't completely happy before and he had been so sure he was. It was the "Who am I?" situation again. He wasn't the guy who was happiest alone anymore.

And then there was the Jack Nicholson thing. "The what?" Elizabeth asked when he tried to explain, because you *can* explain things like that to your best friend.

"You know, the movie with—what's her name and the dog. He won the Oscar?"

"Oh," she said, "*As Good As It Gets*?"

"Yes. I feel like that, like Jack Nicholson."

"What? Obsessive-compulsive?"

"No," he said and smiled. She was very attractive when she was being dense. "You make me want to be a better man."

And she *laughed*. "Nobody's better than you, Christopher," she said. "You're perfect the way you are."

But of course he wasn't. He wanted to be more responsible, to get a reliable job with benefits, so he could support her properly. "You can't get a job that would interfere with your music," she said. "You have a real gift. We would be happy starving in a garret as long as we have each other and your music."

"But security," he said. "Medical insurance."

"Security is overrated," she said. "I like to live dangerously. Besides, I'll get medical insurance on my job."

"Your parents probably want you to marry a rich doctor," he said.

"Not that I care very much what they want," she said, "but my mom always told me to marry for love, and my dad will just be glad you're not a drug addict or an ex-con. No, he'll be happiest that you have a decent haircut. My high school boyfriend's hair was longer than mine—and mine was longer then. It freaked my dad out. He practically danced a jig when we broke up."

"Why did you break up?" he asked, because he couldn't resist, and you can ask your best friend anything.

"He cheated on me," she said. "You won't cheat on me, will you?"

"Never in a million years," he said. Only a longhaired high school geek would cheat on a girl like this.

"She's a gem," Vanessa told him. "Don't let her get away."

"If you don't marry her," his mother said, "I'll have to adopt her."

No one, it seemed, had any doubts, except Christopher.

Oh, he was happy to have this wonderful woman in his life. But in private moments, he worried that the relationship was not real, was not his. Surely she would very soon tire of the person he was trying to become. What she found attractive, even romantic now, in the first blush of new love, would eventually disappoint, grate, repulse. If he was no longer the happy loner, he was not necessarily the man who could live happily ever after with his dream girl. Who exactly was Christopher Reisner?

"You should marry someone like Keith," he told Elizabeth.

"Oh, ugh," she said. "He's so boring." Keith was not boring; he was a standup guy, worthy of beloved Amy. Christopher's eyes did tend to glaze over when Keith talked about investments, but it was his failing, not Keith's. What was it in Elizabeth that could not recognize Keith's merits and imagined a romantic ideal in a penniless composer?

She claimed she never lied—she said remembering who you told which lie was too complicated, and there was always the risk that you might not be believed when you told the truth—so he was surprised when, after telling his mother she wanted two children, a boy and a girl, she told him she didn't want children and never had.

"It's not rocket science," she said. "Your mother is satisfied; she will never ask again. She'll tell anybody else who thinks it's their business. Nobody will pressure me. If they believe I want them, they'll assume it's not my fault if it never happens. It's like a pre-emptive strike."

"It's still a lie," he said.

"It's the exception that proves the rule."

"Are there any more exceptions?" he asked.

"I didn't lie to you," she said, "and I never will. Scout's honor."

He sighed, but not because he didn't believe her. If he could believe she loved him, nothing else could strain credulity. "Why do you put up with me?" he asked, trusting that whatever nonsense she came up with would be true, at least for her.

"Oh!" she said. "I found this poem yesterday, and it made me think of you." She searched through her purse, adding confidingly, "Of course everything makes me think of you."

Christopher knew the feeling well.

Elizabeth found the piece of paper she was hunting for and unfolded it with an air of great ceremony. "It's about giving up smoking,'" she said.

"But I don't smoke," he protested.

"Neither do I," she agreed. "But the author did, and she quit." She handed it to him and watched eagerly while he read it. "Isn't it great? Don't you love that?!"

He supposed it was the musical reference that reminded her of him, but the overall sentiment made him blush. "I do believe you'd prefer me to a cigarette," Christopher said and pulled her onto his lap. "Elizabeth, I have something to tell you that I've never told anybody else. I wouldn't even tell my therapist, if I had one. I wouldn't blame you if you took up smoking after I tell you this."

"Oh, gosh," she said, smiling. "Did you kill somebody?"

"Not yet," he said. "I'm serious. This is something that might change your mind about who I am."

"Shoot," she said.

He told her about his feelings for Amy. What had always felt perfectly natural sounded crazy in the telling. He started to sweat.

"Oh, Christopher," she said when he was finished. "That is so sweet!" Sweet? Not pathetic? Not deranged? Not sort of stalkerish? "To think she settled for a lunkhead like Keith!"

"Keith is great," he said. "Did you ever…?"

"What? Unrequited love? Well, there was Ed Sheeran."

"Are you going to make me sorry I told you?" he asked.

"No—I know it's not the same thing—but it sort of is too."

"Will you get weird with Amy now, or be jealous of her?"

"Only if you get weird with Ed Sheeran."

He sighed. He was almost getting used to his life being turned upside down. "Elizabeth…"

"What, sweetie?"

"Will you marry me?"

"Yeah, I will," she said, simply, casually. "Quickly, before Amy gets a divorce."

She didn't even mind that he hadn't gone down on one knee and offered her a ring. Maybe he didn't have to be a better person to have a better life. Or not better, but different. Who was Christopher Reisner? He was a man who had learned something he'd thought he already knew: There's more than one way to be happy.

"Now," Elizabeth said, "about the lie I told your mother…"

He wasn't very surprised. "Was it a lie?" he asked.

"Yes," she said. "I only want one, and only if he or she will be like you."

Unexpected Love: Chase Allen
by

Anna Lores

Chapter One

Rubbing his weary eyes, Chase Allen forced his shoulders to relax. He couldn't avoid the trip any longer. He promised his stepfather Maverick Cummings a visit. The man wanted a son and surprisingly latched onto him as soon as he found out, after the wedding, that the new love of his life, Lily Champlain, had given life to one.

But leaving his farm to travel two thousand miles to visit a mother he'd seen less than a handful of times since she left his father made his head hurt. He wasn't close to her, proximity or otherwise. The last road trip to Lily's had been a semi-disaster, and ever since—

A car door shut outside.

His border collie Mac shifted in his sleep and slid his head over Chase's cowboy boot and sighed.

With a long exhale, Chase dragged his hands down his cheeks and leaned forward. His elbows landed on the counter of his empty desk. *I need to go. I have to go. It's the right thing to do. The farm can get by without me for a week or, worse case scenario, two.*

The familiar tired shuffle of boots over concrete had him straightening up his spine. *You shouldn't be here so late to check up on me.*

"What's eating you, son?" The gentle yet commanding voice of his father, Kelbie Allen, cut through Chase's thoughts and went straight to the issue he'd been avoiding.

"I don't have this tractor running yet. I've got to fix the fence near the gate. There are two pecan trees that need to come down. The grain silo needs tending. I need to meet with O'Malley about the soil sample and possibly growing a crop of soybeans instead of wheat on the land I'm in negotiations to buy…" *Maverick wants me to stay with him and mother. He doesn't know what she did to me. He doesn't know how much she hates you for getting her pregnant and having to birth me.*

"Those things can wait. I'd go with you, but…" his dad's voice faded into silence like it always did when *she* was involved.

"It wasn't your fault. I was there." Chase's voice softened as he lifted his head and focused his attention on the man who always had his back, no matter what.

"You were five. It was my fault. I shouldn't have been so hard on her and maybe she wouldn't have done what she did. I should have tried harder." His father's lips flattened to a straight line and his gaze drifted to the stained concrete floor.

"She left us both." *Thank God, she left us or I'd be dead and she'd somehow convince the world you did it, not her.* "We ceased to exist as soon as her foot hit the pedal of the new red convertible that you got stuck paying for. Not an ounce of what that woman did could be blamed on you."

Kelbie tilted his head this way and that. The man couldn't argue with the truth.

The woman hadn't contacted them for years. No cards. Nothing, until she married an idiot who wanted to see what kind of offspring she had made with a regular guy. Obnoxious calls from mostly unknown celebrity husbands one, two, and three who were determined to make sure the rednecks from Georgia wouldn't cause problems for them in the media. The woman married men whose chief concern remained their image, just like her.

She had called Dad for help out of a bad situation once in twenty years, and they went to help. It was the only time in his life where she had seemed genuinely humble. They moved her into a hotel in the middle of the night. By the morning, she'd moved on to someone else who could move her up the career chain. No thank-you. No apologies. Nothing from her but the dust kicking up from the wheels of her car as she drove off to another bigger city.

"It's water under the bridge, son. I don't need you to fight my battles, especially the ones that have long been over. Your mother needs a farmer, whether she realizes it or not, to do what needs getting done, and she sure doesn't want me there."

She doesn't want me there—her husband does. "It sounds more like a matchmaking scheme than bonding with her new husband," Chase grumbled.

Deep laughter vibrated the metal walls of the shop.

"Oh yeah. Maverick's version of Cupid games." His laughter instantly died, and a darker tone of truth rose to the surface as his voice lowered. "Lily said Maverick gets what he wants, and he wants you to live there and work for him."

The twitch of his father's cheek and the slight hunch of his shoulders hit Chase in the gut, sending him tumbling into the past memories of his childhood. Lily's hateful words. The blank look of loss and despair in his father's eyes so long ago replayed like a nightmare in his mind.

The ominous call from Grandpa. Dad's smiling lips suddenly sullen and straight. The bright blue of his eyes glazed over into a glassy haze. The rushed movements. Luggage thrown haphazardly in the backseat of the convertible. Mom's green-eyed glare.

"I will tell everyone anything I have to in order to leave with my reputation intact. Your life will be over in this God forsaken town. I'm calling the police. You're not—"

"No one would ever believe it. Doc Prichard would be a witness, Lily. Let me help you. You need help, not running away. My mama takes care of Chase, now. You can focus on getting your head straight. No one knows what you did. You were out of your mind like you are right—"

She lifted her wrists up. Red marks. Faded bruises more green than blue or purple. "Should I show you my ankles?" The actress in her came out in every word, every tone change, every fake stumble. "I'll take Chase and beat the shit out of him again. I'll do more than cut him. And I'll record him saying you did it. I'll force him to name you. Who would the world believe, me?" She whimpered and tears flooded her eyes. She dropped the façade as her expression fell flat. "Or you?"

Chase's heartbeat tripled as the memories flooded his system.

The evil woman grabbed Chase by the neck. He thrashed as her hands constricted, cutting off his oxygen. Dad grabbed him from her and pulled him up into his arms. "Go. Take what you want. I'm keeping my boy, safe. You're never gonna hurt him again."

Fear of never seeing his father again, of never stepping foot on Georgia soil for the rest of his life, of being with a mother who assaulted him, shook him to his very core as much that day as it had all those years ago.

Dad tucked Chase behind him, protecting him from the woman who should have loved them both.

Stiletto heels stomped on the cracked Georgia clay. The drought had taken its toll on the land and, in turn, their finances.

Dad's enormous back expanded as his arm and hand held Chase close against his back. "The entire town knows you have a lover in the city. Run, but you can't—"

"I can do anything I want. You're a sick sonofabitch, and that is what I'll tell anyone who asks why I left."

Chase's stomach twisted and turned as bile crept up his esophagus.

Water spilled over the bridge that day. Hell, a damn hundred-foot tidal wave swept away the bridge and everyone on it.

Mac's muzzle pushed at Chase's hand.

"Hey, look at me," his father whispered.

The impenetrable fortress of the man protecting him from the woman who wanted to take him away to hurt his father slowly faded, and the bright blue eyes and stoic face he counted on every day came into focus.

"Son, it's going to be fine. You're strong. You own your own business. You don't need her or him or me or anyone. Let them think you're just a man trying to work the land. They don't know anything about you that you haven't told them. And they're too lazy to actually do any research about you."

Yeah. They don't know I have more money than husband number six, Maverick Cummings. Only you and

Granny and Pappy know my net worth. "Granny came by, hugging and kissing me and acting like I'm never coming back home. She filled up the hunting cooler. I have enough food to feed an army."

"Have you looked at yourself lately?"

"Are you saying I'm fat?" Chase stood up and patted his chest and belly. He towered over his father's six foot frame.

"You're a fucking brick house." With a sizeable grin, his dad turned on his boot heels and walked past the antique tractor Chase had been tinkering with for weeks. "I'll get your tractor ready."

"No, sir. I'll do it when I get back. Just take care of my horse and business while I'm gone." He grabbed his jacket and followed his father to the gray steel door entrance to the open garage hangar, with Mac heeling beside him.

"I won't call unless something serious pops up," his dad said.

"Call with minor issues, Dad. You know how I am." *I'm just like you. I like to control everything.* He switched off the lights and closed up shop.

His father pushed open the steel door, and the first surge of a winter cold system blasted them in the face. Dad zipped up his jacket over his heavily starched western shirt and shoved his hands in his pockets. "You packing a business shirt and tie in case Maverick wants to take you to his office and show off?"

"Yes, sir. Granny walked in while I was packing and took over. She packed my bags with all kinds of clothes. And she added blizzard kits for me and Mac and a crate full of shit I'll never use. She even packed a snowboard. I didn't have the heart to tell her Lily moved again and there isn't snow or a ski resort where I'm going."

"There's no telling what that man has in store for you this time of year. I'm sure you got them all in a tizzy over driving instead of flying on their private jet."

"Yes, sir." Refusing Maverick's gifts caused some hard feelings, but gifts from those people were payment for something they hadn't gotten yet. He wasn't about to owe anything to anyone, especially not them. Driving down an open road meant control and allowed him the ability to leave at any moment. Day. Or. Night.

Following his father's confident steps, Chase's anxiety increased. As soon as his father drove off, he'd begin the long drive west with his faithful companion Mac. *No more procrastinating.*

He stopped as his father climbed into a gunmetal heavy-duty work truck.

"You'll have plenty of time to take a vacation," his dad said. "If you want to join a sightseeing tour somewhere along the way—or not-so-along the way, do it. I'll be here when you get home."

"I have a farm to run. I need to be here."

"You need to get laid. You're wound up tighter than a pissed off rattlesnake."

"Are you trying to run me off?" *I should tell you I'm still a virgin. After what Lily did, I'd have to fall so deeply in love that my mind would slow down and focus solely on making her fall in love with me. And that hasn't happened, yet. Probably never will.*

Amusement seemed to play in his father's eyes, bright with life once again. A lopsided grin formed on his face. "Show those two how a real man does things. Don't take any of their shit and make whatever you're building as strong as the State of Georgia."

He nodded, clamping his jaw down tight. *Ain't nothing that strong.* "I'll do my best to represent you, me, and Georgia well while I'm there."

His father's laughter echoed outside until it was silenced by the car door shutting.

Yep, riling me up on purpose, making me wish I hadn't agreed to go. But I need to see if Mother has changed. I think that kind of evil in a person doesn't just go away, no matter what the preacher says.

The engine revved.

In seconds, Chase stepped back with Mac beside him, and watched his father's pickup truck back out of the parking area and head up the gravel drive toward the road.

He glanced at the pecan orchard at the front of his property hiding his white southern plantation home from the road. He looked over his shoulder and gazed at his workshop and the surrounding fields that went on for miles. The land didn't look like much this time of year, but hidden underneath the nutrient rich soil was the magical seed of life that, come spring, would sprout beautiful golden stalks of wheat to harvest in late May or early June.

He walked to his truck parked in the drive on the side of his house. *I can always leave. If she tries to...* He held his stomach and Mac pushed firmly against his side, pulling him out of the thought patterns that sent him down a path to panic. "Thanks, boy. I guess we ought to go, so we can hurry and get back home." *Five days of work with Maverick. I can handle anything for five days, even the woman who stars in my worst nightmares.*

Chapter Two

Slicing lemons for the nonexistent crowd they expected tonight seemed like a waste of time, but Zoe Burke cut through the yellow rind into the acidic juicy segments anyway.

The sleigh bells hanging on the doorknob jingled.

"Welcome to—" She started the regular greeting but halted as her brother Declan Burke, the manager and owner of Burke's Bar, shook the rain from his coat as he walked over the threshold. "Burke's Bar."

He stepped on the entry mat and body checked the door to close it all the way. "You still graduating tomorrow?"

"You still breathing?" She balled up a clean towel and threw it as hard as she could toward him.

He stepped off the mat and caught it.

She gazed at the sliced lemon pieces. *I can't believe I will have my Masters in Psychology diploma in my hand tomorrow.*

He chuckled as he took off his blue raincoat and placed it on a hook near the door. "I am breathing, Miss Summa Cum Laud-ass."

She raised her gaze enough to see the only person who ever genuinely loved her wiping the wet floor where his flip flops had made a slippery mess. He raised his gaze and held a barely-there-grin on his face.

"Har. Har." She rolled her eyes at him, inciting the

small curve of his lips to form a larger smile. His bright blue eyes sparkled, seemingly with pride, and his stride took him straight toward her.

Changing gears, she wiped her hands, grabbed a tumbler, and filled it with ice and cola. She placed it on the pristine wooden bar counter and topped it with a slice of fresh lemon. "For the best brother in the entire world and beyond."

He dropped his butt into the leather bar chair. His joyous smile faded to a flat line. "Thanks."

She nodded and took in a deep breath. *Truth time. Did we get the answer to our prayers?* She exhaled frustration. "So?"

"The offer was low, but doable. If the beer festival was now, I wouldn't even consider selling the bar at this price. But, it's not, and I'm not taking out a loan to float this place again. We can finally walk away from all the baggage Mom and Dad left us with and start over."

She swallowed hard. *It isn't just their baggage we need to get away from. Pieces of mine still cling to me.*

"Is there enough to open up a bar or restaurant someplace else? Maybe someplace warm? A small town that needs a local bar and grill?" Her heart stopped beating. Her lungs quit taking in oxygen. *There has to be enough. Please, please, please, let there be enough for you to follow your dreams too.*

He shook his head. His fingers trailed the base of the glass as the sparkling bubbles floated up to the rim in the dark syrup.

"I doubt it. I'd have to make improvements upstairs. I'd need free supplies. If I had some tile to fix that floor, I could renegotiate the contract and have enough money left over to buy a fixer-upper restaurant in a small town in need of great food at an affordable price. As it is right now, the offer will get us out with a little cushion, but buying our own business probably isn't possible. If Mom and Dad hadn't burned the…" He inhaled and sighed. "We'd need a damn miracle to walk through that door."

"We could apply for a loan wherever we land. If one of the jobs I applied for in the Southeast works out—"

The jingle of bells drew her gaze from her brother's sullen slouch to the entrance of the bar.

An enormous figure in a bright orange rain jacket stood half-inside and half-outside the doorway.

Scanning upward, she saw a shadow of light brown stubble on a strong jaw of a man whose instant presence put her at ease and riled her up at the same time. An innocent indention of dimples on his cheeks moved her exploration farther. Full lips made her long to hear his voice giving her a sexy greeting. A gentlemanly quality about his posture pushed her to lean forward to catch any sliver of information that he might offer about himself.

Lust formed a sudden wet barrier between her thoughts and her panties. His freckled nose drew her gaze upward to the most soulful caramel eyes. *You're a man I can trust.*

"Ma'am, can I bring my dog inside?" The deep southern drawl of the man's voice sent ripples of desire rushing through her veins.

Yes. She nodded fervently. *You can bring anything you want in.* Her mouth wouldn't work, but the rest of her body perked up and screamed for him to come in and stay a while.

"We're closed," Declan said. "But bring your dog in out of the rain. Have a drink with us."

Tugging slightly at the tip of his weathered brown

cowboy hat, he nodded. His dark gaze kept her waiting, on edge, for him to say something, anything. *Who are you and why are you here?*

"Thanks." The man took off his jacket and hung it on the hook next to Declan's. He pushed the door close and tilted his head to the side and stared at it for a moment. He opened and lifted it a hair. "Hmm." He swung it an inch in and out. He bent down and looked at the lock. A ball of black and white fur moved under his jacket and sat. The man reached into his pocket and drew out an army knife. He checked the door, made some kind of adjustment, and stood up. He closed the door and it clicked. He opened it again and closed it softly. Open. Close. Open. Close. The door clicked like it should for the first time since she could remember. He turned the deadbolt and nodded.

He took off his hat and ran his fingers through the thick brown waves of curls on his head. He flipped the lock open, pivoted on his heel, and sauntered forward in a swagger like he was the boss. He seemed too comfortable in the bar. He seemed like he was used to being stared at, respected, obeyed.

You are not from here with that sexy mumbling drawl. And I'm not playing games. I don't need to think about love when—

The gaze compelling her to wait for his next words shifted focus to her brother, releasing her from his silent hold.

She sucked in a lungful of air. Her heart started pumping again, but in a fevered frenzy of beats. Something was seriously wrong with her. She hadn't been interested in a man since Talin, and he turned into a jerk.

The shuffle and hard heel strike of cowboy boots and the padding of paws over the wooden floors thundered in her ears as if he were telling her he was coming for her, only her.

Something about his stride had her wishing she could tell him all her secrets, her desires, her fears. With him, she would have nowhere to hide, no other choice but to offer the truth and hope he would accept her. She would fall in love...and he would walk away, like everyone else had when they found out about her past.

"I'm Declan Burke. This is my sister, Zoe."

"Hey, I'm Chase Allen, from Farmers Chapel, Georgia." He placed his hat on the seat of the corner bar chair. His hand engulfed Declan's as they shook in greeting.

"You're bigger than Declan," she gasped. Her flesh turned to fire as the words she'd spoken sank in. Chase Allen was bigger and stronger and more confident than the strongest and biggest and most confident man she'd ever known—her brother.

The man's lips turned up into a grin that validated what he was—a confident man.

No ring on your finger. Working man's hands. What do you do? She swallowed, hoping to get her body to cool down, but it told her to go and deny her feelings to someone else. Her cheeks flamed with embarrassment as if he knew every inch of her was responding inappropriately to him. And she was pretty sure he did know or at least noticed with the way her skin suddenly burned and glistened with perspiration.

"And you're a little thing, Zoe." He slipped out of a gray thermal shirt and revealed a black tee hugging his chest like it was thrilled to be there and would fight her off to stay connected to his flesh.

"You're not like most men," she mumbled too loudly. *I can barely form two words with you, and now I can't shut up?* She forced her lips closed. But the genuineness in his eyes made her want to open up and tell him everything, even the most miserable parts of her life.

"You're right. I'm not like most men. I'm a farmer. There's only about two percent of us in the United States."

Her lips parted to take in a puff of the air surrounding him. "I bet you're great at growing things." *God, I'm an idiot. I need help to communicate normally with him. Is this love at first sight? Is this sensation what it feels like to fall in love?*

"Zoe, give the guy a drink." Declan's voice knocked her out of whatever mindscrew she was in with hot and sexy farmer Chase Allen.

"Oh, yeah. Sorry." *It's not like I'm going to marry the man. I doubt there is a man alive who would marry me after I tell him about my history.* She shook her head and grabbed a glass tumbler. "What do you want?" *Please don't ask for a beer. No. Ask for a beer. Fantasy farmer will end with your order. No alcoholics. No drug addicts. No heavy partiers. I want a man who is responsible, loving, nurturing, supportive. I need a man who will pass Declan's man-worth-my-time test.*

"A cola would be great."

Thank you, God. A soda drinker. Her hands trembled as she added ice and cola to the glass. *Calm down. Calm down. He's just a man. He's passing through. He's not interested, and I'm living next to Declan for the rest of my life. We're a package deal.*

She placed the glass down in front of him.

"Breathe, sweetheart." Chase leaned forward toward her. His voice lowered to a soft whisper. "I grow things. Fix things. No need to be nervous."

"Yeah, uh, thanks for whatever you did with the door." She inhaled. His words lingered in her ears—"*I grow things, fix things." Can you fix me?*

Her hands continued to tremble with the kind of want that would keep her up all night wishing he was with her—holding her under his firm control, whispering he needed her, that she gave him everything he ever wanted in a woman, but wishing more than anything that he loved her.

She wetted her lips and attempted to raise her gaze from the perfectly shaped muscles filling out his chest and neck. *Those biceps and forearms and hands. I'd suck on your fingertips. Kiss the pulse at your taut neck. I'd...no. No thoughts of intimacies or love or marriage or babies with fantasy farmer. But I want all that with my fantasy farmer. This might really be love.*

She moaned softly.

Declan raised his brow at her and turned toward their guest. "Uh, Chase, what brings you here?"

Quickly, she cleared her throat and ignored the areas that were throbbing but shouldn't have been. "Yeah, uh…Are you passing through? Visiting for a day or two or week or more? Is there a farming conference nearby we don't know about? Are you moving here?"

Chase's tongue traced his lips in what seemed to be a call to action for her to lean in for a taste.

"Visiting," he said in that sexy drawl. "I'm doing some kind of renovation for, or with, or heck, I don't know what I'm in for. Why my latest stepfather hasn't hired someone, I don't know." He settled into the bar chair next to Declan as if he'd known them forever and planned to catch up on everything, including her, since the last time they were together. "I think it's his first renovation, and I'll just say it without guilt. He's a damn idiot. I'm on my way there, but..." The timbre of his voice changed, softened as if he were struggling with something he wanted to get off his chest, yet couldn't.

"You haven't seen him in a long time, and you need some more down time before you have to be 'on' for the rest of your visit. Am I close?" *Only, you're having a soda instead of a beer to get ready for an uncomfortable situation. Not drowning your sorrows like most patrons.*

"Try the first time I've met him," he mumbled. "He and my mother live nearby. Maverick Cummings and Lily Champlain. Do you know them?"

The confidence in his brown eyes wavered, showing an insecurity she often saw in the patients that came to the psychology clinic where she interned and in the customers that sat down at the bar counter to drink their lives away.

You're afraid of something? Someone? What or who would frighten a man like you? Zoe reached forward, her heart aching to comfort him, ease whatever seemed to be bothering him. But she stopped before she touched his arm. She didn't need to follow her desire to be closer to him, to ease whatever was worrying him. She worked hard every day to turn off that side of her, turn off the side that wanted to help everyone she came in contact with. Turn off the side of her that wanted to do more than listen to him. Turn off the obedient side. The side that got her nothing but a broken heart and ego, and then discarded like trash.

Declan's bar chair squeaked, interrupting her thoughts of the farmer wreaking havoc on her emotions.

"I don't know your mother Lily, but I do know Maverick," Declan said. "You're the son he's never had but always wanted, aren't you?"

Chase lifted the tumbler that seemed more like a child's sippy cup in his large hand and brought it to his lips. He nodded. "Yup." His lips curled around the side of the rim while a vulnerability opened up within his gaze. He gulped most of the beverage down as she fell deeper and deeper into a place she hadn't allowed her heart or mind to go since she got released from outpatient rehab seven years ago.

Curiosity and chemistry tugged at her to get closer, ask questions, dig deeper, find out everything about the man with an unhealed, secret wound hidden deep within his heart.

Hesitant to open her mouth, not knowing what would come out—the counselor or the love starved woman, she gave in to her curiosity and words tumbled off her tongue. "They got married six months ago, and you're just coming to meet him *now*?" *Did you fight with your mother? You don't approve of him? You're worried and want to protect her?*

He placed the glass on the counter and lowered his gaze. "Found out she got married when the husband called me out of the blue. Dad used to build and renovate houses on the side. We had a business doing that for a while. Dude's been burning up my damn line since he found out I existed. I just want to get this over with and get back to my farm. That's it. But no, Maverick just told me the tile I picked up in New Mexico isn't what Lily wants now, so I got a truckload of tile and…" He continued telling them about an oversized-bathroom project that now wasn't a bathroom project but an in-law cottage project with a dumpster which couldn't go on their property because of some issue he didn't have time to work through.

"I'm doing some renovations upstairs. If the stuff you bought is neutral colored and simple to install, I'll buy it from you," Declan offered. "And, you can put the construction dumpster behind the bar."

"I'll give you the tile, if you're serious about allowing the dumpster on your property." The shimmer of a twinkle appeared in Chase's eyes.

"I know the owner of the only dumpster company in the area. I'll take care of it." Declan grabbed his phone from his front pocket and tapped the screen. "It's no big deal. Glad to help out."

"If you need any help around here, I'm eight miles away at a bed and breakfast." His gaze shifted to her.

"It sounds more like you're the one that might need some help," she said. Butterflies fluttered in her belly at the prospect of seeing the farmer again. *If the dumpster is in the back of the bar, I will be seeing a lot of you, Chase Allen.*

"Where do you want me to unload the tile?" His dark eyes seemed to shine like freshly polished amber.

"By the back entrance," she whispered. "Do you need help?"

"Not with the tile. Hand me your phone and I'll give you my contact information."

On autopilot, she handed it over. Her surprisingly steady fingers brushed the calloused palm of his hand in a hesitant retreat. His thumbs swiftly typed his name and number into her contacts.

Drawing the phone down below the bar counter, hiding the screen, he continued to type into her phone.

She leaned forward, trying to get a glimpse of the phone screen. *Why so secretive?*

"The dumpster is getting dropped off today." Declan interrupted her attempt at spying.

"Thanks, Declan." Chase placed her phone face down on the counter next to his half-empty glass of soda and stood.

"No problem." Declan's fingers softly tapped the edge of the bar in the rhythm of a song she recognized but couldn't place.

"I've got to get going." Chase stayed sitting, silently staring at her for a long few seconds.

"She's single," Declan said.

She tore her focus from the man with the ability to mesmerize her with one look and gave Declan her best I'm-gonna-kill-you glare.

"Declan." *You're my brother not my dating manager.* Her cheeks blazed with a deeper heat, one that came from a place she couldn't ignore around Chase— the place that kept nagging her to show him just how much she liked him.

"What?" Declan shrugged, unfazed. His gaze drifted to Chase's and then back to hers. "You are single. Very single. *Extremely single* and *available*."

She pressed her hand to her forehead. "Oh God," she groaned.

"Are you busy tomorrow night?" Chase's sexy drawl snuck past layers of fortified defenses surrounding her heart.

Her mouth dropped open and her eyes had to have bugged out by the seemingly amused expression lifting the corners of Chase's lips. But his eyes trapped her the way she wanted to be trapped—by someone who understood her desire to trust and love a good man.

Not at all. Not busy. Never busy. I'd go out with you in a heartbeat. I'd bail on the ceremony tomorrow afternoon to go anywhere with... Gathering her senses, she straightened her spine and inhaled. "I'm busy."

"No, you're not." Declan stood up next to Chase. The larger-than-life brother who always protected her wasn't so large compared to the farmer.

"It's cool." Chase grabbed his coat and pulled it on. "It's a woman's prerogative to decline a date request. My offer to help y'all still stands. I'll unload the tile now and leave it in the back. It was nice meeting you." He reached into the inside pocket of his jacket and pulled out an expensive but worn leather wallet. He took out some bills and held it out to Declan.

"Your soda is on me." Declan held out his hand to shake. "Stop by any time. You and your dog are always welcome here."

Chase shook his hand. "Thanks." He strode toward the door with his dog obediently heeling at his side. He slipped into his rain jacket. The bells jingled as he opened the door.

Something so primal inside her panicked with his feet so close to the exit. *Don't go. I've changed my mind. I'll go out with you. This time, I'll be honest.*

"Bye, Chase," flew from her lips instead of the words she wanted to say. *Look at me like you want me one more time.*

He glanced over his shoulder and nodded. "Bye, Zoe."

She lifted her hand and waved. A thin thread of joy

seemed to rush from her, wrap around him, and bind her to him.

A grin spread across his face, but he turned around and walked out of the bar and out of her life, breaking their fragile new bond.

"Why didn't you say 'yes' to him?" Declan asked.

She scooped up Chase's glass and began cleaning it. *Too scared. My past is too problematic. People say they can deal with my past, but they can't. I can't.* "A man like that doesn't want a girl like me."

Declan's hand gripped her forearm and stopped her from rinsing the soap from the glass. "You stop that. What happened to you is over. It's in the past. A good man appreciates a good woman, and you're the best damn woman I've ever known. I'm lucky to have you as my sister."

She nodded, but he was wrong. A man like Chase Allen wouldn't want an ex-junkie as a wife, lover, girlfriend, or even a friend. It didn't matter that she'd been clean for seven years. It didn't matter she got hooked on drugs because her parents decided they wanted to party and the only one available to supply their habit was their preteen daughter—her. It didn't matter they threatened her, guilted her, punished her, used her. She had done what she had to do back then. She would have done anything to survive. Absolutely. Anything. And she had.

"You like that guy. Take some of your own advice and believe in the ability of others to accept you as the wonderful person you are. Go out on one date with him." He lifted her hand and placed his other hand on top, sandwiching hers.

"He won't ask again, and I'm not going to ask him

on a date." *He only stopped in because he needed a place for a dumpster, and we are the only business that has the space for something like that.*

She dropped her shoulders and pressed her lips together. *I should have accepted the date. But I'm not up for dating another domineering man like the last one. Nice guy until he found out I was 'that' ex-junkie.* "Let's sign that contract and—"

"Don't think I don't know what you're doing. I'll let it go for now, but we will get back to you and your love life. Since we have use of a free dumpster and some free tile, we're going to look into repairing some of the fire damage upstairs to bring in a better price. Depending on the tile Chase is unloading, we could tile the bathroom floor upstairs. The realtor gave me a list of items that would increase the value, and the buyer would be interested in negotiating a higher price." He let go of her hand, wiped his wet hands on his jeans, and gazed at the counter.

"Huh? Chase left his hat. I guess you'll have to call him." He raised his left eyebrow and angled his head to the side. "He is into you, sis."

"He's not *into me.* He left it by accident." She wiped her hands on the bar towel next to the sink beside her. She picked up her phone from the counter and typed in her password. The message screen popped up. *Chase Allen.*

—Keep my hat until you have an opening in your calendar to spend some time with me. Only then, call me. For anything else, have your brother call.—

Oh. My. God. Her hand shook as she showed Declan the note.

The slightest hint of wrinkles formed at the corners

of his eyes as he read the text. He handed the phone back to her. "Well? What are you going to do?"

"I'm not calling." She walked to the end of the bar and ducked under instead of lifting the broken-hinged section. *We're going to have to fix the counter before we sell this place.* "I'm not interested in—"

The bells jingled.

Chase? She popped up next to Declan and twirled to see who caused the noise.

The old man who owned the florist shop a few stores down shuffled in with a bouquet of crimson roses. He continued forward, his focus on Declan.

"These are for her. The man paid cash and wrote the note himself." He handed a small envelope to her brother. Keeping his gaze on Declan, the man extended his arm with the vase of fragrant, blooming, red roses at her.

"They're beautiful," she whispered. She inhaled, taking in the sweet-smelling aroma. Declan had been the only person to ever buy her flowers, and he always bought her orange tiger lilies because they reminded him of her hair.

"The man wasn't from here. Now, she's been good for a long time, but we don't want any problems with transients. He paid in cash. And he had a lot of it." He tucked his chin against his chest, turned the corner of his lips down into a deep frown, and raised his white eyebrows. "If you know what I mean."

I can't stay here. No matter what I do, I'll always be the junkie whore who survived the fire.

"He's visiting his family from here. There is no *problem*. Zoe has been clean and sober for seven years. She's—" Declan's face turned red and his nostrils flared with a deep inhalation. "Mr. Winters, the man you met is a nice guy. Because a man you don't know sends my sister flowers does not mean he is on drugs, sells drugs, or has anything to do with drugs."

Mr. Winters' frown deepened. He turned around and walked out the way he came mumbling, "I'm warning you. That's all."

Declan ripped open the note as the bells jingled with Mr. Winter's exit.

"Chase hopes you like the roses even though these aren't fresh. He says you're more beautiful than the Georgia sunrise over a harvest of golden wheat." Declan chuckled. "I think I'm in love."

"I smell a bromance brewing," she quipped. *Mr. Chase Allen, you're the kind of man I'd follow down any road. But I'm not doing that. I'm not going anywhere without my brother. Ever.*

"You have to call him. If you don't, I will. And I'll set you up on a date with him at an ungodly hour in the morning." He one-arm side-hugged her, tucking her under his protective wing.

"I don't want Chase to…People talk. I'm…" She inhaled and closed her mouth as she exhaled. Fear drove too many of her choices. "If Mr. Winters saw me out with Chase, he'd find Chase's mother and tell her about me. Even if Chase could overlook my past, chances are his family couldn't."

"Mr. Winters is a jerk. The other shop owners are nice. They all like and trust you. They—"

She turned and wrapped her arms around him, hugging him tightly. "You're right. This is a good community of people. It's me. It's me that needs to get away from the ghosts of those who died, from the nightmares of years of being strung out, from the streets and corners that I slept in, that I cross every day. It's me, Declan. I can't get away from the bad memories *haunting me* everywhere I turn."

"Zoe…" The encouraging lecture that usually followed didn't happen. He kissed the top of her head. "Let's check out that tile and see if it will work for the floor. If I can get Selena to help, I could get it installed in two days. We'll close at the end of the month and be starting over someplace where no one has ever heard of Burke's Bar or the fire. In the meantime, you have a thank-you call to make and a farmer to invite over for dinner."

The Cowboy and the Lady
by

Jean Adams

Chase Brand pushed his white Stetson to the back of his head, and was scanning the passengers as they came through the gate when he saw the blonde beauty. She looked lost as she came through the Arrivals concourse. Was this her?

The one with her nose in the air. The one who looked like she was staring down every man in the airport terminal. It was no more than he'd expected, given her background. Had to be.

Lady Laura Davenport, that was her name, and his boss had given him strict instructions to call her "Your Ladyship." Hell, did he look halfway decent to be Her Ladyship's meet and greet? He'd been honored to be chosen as her wrangler for the next two weeks. Now he wasn't so sure.

Wow! She was a stunner though, with strawberry blonde hair drawn back into a ponytail. He hoped she didn't expect too much of him.

He pushed his fingers through his hair before replacing his Stetson, then pulled a piece of white card that read "Davenport" in big black letters from under his arm, and held it above his head. She noticed the card the moment he held it aloft and started toward him with the most beautiful smile he'd ever seen. It almost knocked him sideways. He hadn't expected anything so enchanting from such a sour-looking face. The smile lit up her whole countenance. It was as though she had brought sunshine with her. Several pairs of male eyes followed her when she started toward him. Who could blame them? Something warm and erotic moved in his stomach. Was he gaping like a loon? *Better stop that. You're only a weather-worn cowboy. She's too good for you.*

"Lady Davenport?" he queried as she approached him. "I'm Chase Brand. Your personal wrangler."

Her smile broadened. "Hello, Chase, but please, call me Laura. And excuse me if I was staring. I can't see too clearly without my glasses. It's okay if I focus, though."

Well, that explained that. She hadn't been staring men down. She'd been looking for him. Made him feel good. Her soft voice kicked him right in the solar plexus. "Laura," he repeated. He just couldn't help himself. It would probably be the only time he'd be permitted to call her that.

"So you're from the Circle Zed. Thank you for meeting me."

"Sure am, and it's my pleasure to meet you, ma'am." And he was the lucky S.O.B. who would get to spend the next two weeks with her.

"Oops. I forgot. It's Circle Zee, isn't it?"

Cute with it. He chuckled. "You call it whatever you want, ma'am. So anytime you want to ride, I saddle the horse for you, as well as look after him, and ride with you, make sure no harm comes to you."

She laughed. "That'll be lovely. But thanks, I'll be okay. I've been riding all my life."

"Still my job to look out for you. Here, let me." He took the baggage trolley from her, pushed it out into the afternoon sunshine, and crossed the car park to where the big guest car was parked. "I'll put your bags in the trunk." He hefted her suitcase into the back and went for the carryall. "Must say, you travel light." Made a man wonder how flimsy her underwear was. Hardly anything of it, he'd like to bet. *Better control thoughts like that, Chase*. He smiled and held open the passenger door. "So, how long are you staying?"

"About two weeks. So, do I call you Chase?"

"Sure."

"I was looking at the scenery as we came in to land. It's beautiful."

"Yeah. It's real pretty, all right."

He wasn't thinking about the scenery. His thoughts were on the way the sunlight caught the strands of her blonde hair. He wondered how that silky hair would play through his fingers if she let it out.

Don't give it any head space, Chase, ol' buddy. You're way out of her league.

"Is the Circle Zee far?" Her melodic voice broke into his thoughts.

He settled into his seat. Two weeks with her wouldn't be as bad as he'd feared. In fact, he might even enjoy it. "About an hour and a half. Real nice drive though, so settle back and relax."

****

Laura bit her lip, hardly able to believe the man sitting beside her.

Relax he'd said. How could she relax with his handsome hunk sitting so close? She glanced at him from the corner of her eyes. Manly profile, soft, dark brown eyes. Beautifully shaped mouth. Good heavens. Everything about him was her idea of a dreamy cowboy.

As a girl, and later, as a young woman, she'd had her heart set on marrying a cowboy, for which her brother teased her mercilessly. Who'd have thought the first one she met would tie her stomach in knots? Were they all like him?

"So, what made you choose the Circle Zee? The horse riding, or the cattle trails?" His soft, husky voice broke into her thoughts.

She gathered her wits. "Lots of reasons. The horse riding, mainly. I love horses. Actually, I love anything western. See all the movies, watch reruns on TV. But mainly because my grandfather knows Mr. Adamson, the senior. They've been good friends since the war."

"Davenport! Of course. I should have recognized the name." He shot her a quick sideways glance. "Ain't he the guy who saved old man Adamson's life during the war? Pushed him out of the way of a sniper, or something, then lay across him to protect him from gunfire 'til they could be rescued?"

"I believe so."

"Your grandpappy's something of a hero around these parts."

"Thank you."

"It's a real pleasure to know you, Miss Davenport. Sorry, I mean, Your Ladyship."

"Please don't bother with all that rigmarole, Chase. Laura suits me fine." She settled comfortably in her seat, and smiled. "And it's a real pleasure to meet you, too. So, how often do we ride?"

"As often as you want. You're the guest, so I follow your orders."

She laughed. "I get to give orders to a sexy cowboy, eh?"

He cleared his throat. "No one's ever called me sexy before."

She never thought she'd ever see a cowboy blush.

"I—I'm sorry. I didn't mean to embarrass you; the words just came out." Too easily. "Anyway, riding will be fairly often, if that's all right with you. I usually try to ride every day."

"Fine with me. And, hey, don't spoil it. For the record, I'm not embarrassed. Just surprised."

During the drive, he entertained her with stories about the Circle Zee. "And on Fridays, there's a picnic at the covered wagons out on the open range."

"Wow! I'll enjoy that."

Chase stopped the car outside a large ranch house at the end of a long, wide driveway. "Here we are. I'll take you in to Mr. Adamson. He's looking forward to seeing you. He'd have come to the airport to meet you, but his wheelchair gets a mite cumbersome." He led her through the big open house into a large foyer and on to a room at the end of a passageway.

Ted Adamson smiled up from his wheelchair and held his arms out in welcome. "Sorry I couldn't get to the airport myself, but it takes me a while to do anything these days."

"That's all right. I was met by a very nice man." She looked around to smile at Chase, but he'd disappeared from the room. Disappointed, she focused her attention on Ted Adamson. After brief hugs, Laura reached into her bag and took out a blue velvet box. "I've brought you something from Granddad."

The old man's eyes teared up when he opened the box and saw the medal inside. "What's this?"

Laura smiled. "It's his Victoria Cross."

"Didn't he want to keep it? For his family?"

"He wanted you to have it," she said gently.

The old man rubbed a hand over his eyes. "Thank

you."

She reached into her bag again. "And this is from me," she said, and took out a bottle of the finest bourbon.

"He never forgets. Sends me a bottle every Christmas."

"So, is this the English girl?" A male voice interrupted their meeting.

It came from behind her. She turned and saw a young man, advancing toward her. He was tall, slim, and very blond, dressed in a fancy light gray suit teamed with a dark gray and red neckerchief. He was very handsome, too handsome for her taste, judging by the way he swaggered across the room.

"Laura, this is my grandson, Steve. Steve, meet Laura."

She reached out to offer her hand. He took it and pressed it to his lips, but there was something unsavory about the touch of his lips on her skin. "Very pretty," was all he said.

The slide of his gaze gave her the shivers. Nevertheless, she offered him a smile in return. It could be all in her imagination. "Thank you."

"So, when I've managed to ditch my guest, I'll be your wrangler."

"I thought Chase was my wrangler."

"The hired help?" He shook his head. "You're to have VIP treatment. You won't get that with the hired help."

"I don't need any red carpet. I'm getting along very nicely with Chase."

Ted Adamson laughed. "Hah! You've finally met a woman who doesn't fall at your feet in gratitude."

Thank goodness Chase was still her personal

wrangler. She was looking forward to riding together for hours on end, having picnics in the shade of the big trees while their horses grazed lazily under wide branches. She gave herself a mental kick. And just maybe she had a few preconceived ideas about what life on a dude ranch would be like.

"Come with me," Steve said. "I'll show you to your cabin."

"Oh, okay." She turned and smiled at Ted. "See you later."

"Dinner's at seven," he called after her.

"She'll be here," Steve called over his shoulder.

Outside the house, Chase waited. He was sitting in a rocking chair looking out over the fields but jumped to his feet the moment she appeared. Her heart gave a little skip at the sight of him, his Stetson pushed to the back of his head, and his hair falling in a black riot over his forehead.

She brightened the moment she saw him. "Hi, Chase."

"All set, Laura, uh, Lady Davenport," he corrected when he saw Steve behind her, and tipped the brim of his hat with one finger.

"You take care of my girl," Steve ordered.

"Your girl?" Chase squared his shoulders and stepped forward as though protecting her. "She'll be in safe hands with me."

"Come Sunday, he's reassigned her to me."

Laura shot a quick glance at Chase. How dare Steve be so rude? She'd nip this in the bud right now. "I didn't hear him say anything about that."

"Well, he meant to, but he's going senile. Besides I'm sure you'd rather be with me than stuck with the

215

hired help."

No! She wouldn't. The hired help was just fine with her. In just a few minutes, and after some arrogant, presumptuous sentences, she'd soon realized Steve's measure. But with Chase she'd got the impression of a perfect gentleman. He talked easily, without pretense or conceit, made her laugh, kept her entertained with a couple of stories. Goodness, how could she have lost an hour and a half with him so quickly? She'd barely noticed the countryside slide by. As far as she was concerned, the drive could have gone on forever.

"Steve! Come here, will you?" It was Ted.

He tutted. "What do want, Grandpaw?"

"You. Here. Now."

Steve huffed out a sigh and stomped along the passageway toward where his grandfather waited in his wheelchair.

"No sense in waiting around," Chase said with a grin. "I'll show you to your cabin."

****

Laura's two weeks passed all too quickly, and now her time was almost up. Only two days left. But she had a problem. She had fallen in love with Chase, and as each day passed, she fell a little bit more in love. She enjoyed the time she spent with him. They rode together every day, even took part in a cattle drive and slept under the stars, which left Laura spellbound. This was what she had expected of western life, and Chase made sure she enjoyed plenty of it.

A knock on her cabin door told her company had arrived, but it didn't sound like Chase's knock. "Come in. The door's open."

"Mornin', sweetcakes."

"Steve!" She swallowed. "Where's Chase?"

"He won't be bothering you anymore."

"He wasn't bothering me. We were going for a good long ride this morning, then on to the covered wagons for lunch."

"Well, you can go with me instead." He reached out and touched her hair.

She managed to disguise a shiver.

"Besides, he's probably packing."

She swallowed. "Packing. Where's he going?"

"He's had enough. Decided to quit. So, you have me as your personal wrangler for your last few days."

"I thought you already had a guest."

"I was able to dump her."

She rolled her eyes. "Charming!"

He grinned. "Thought you'd be pleased."

"Your grandfather assigned Chase to me."

"The old man wouldn't know if his backside was on fire. Shall we go?"

He smiled as he led her out of the door toward the stables.

Chase appeared leading two horses. Her heart did double a flip. His lean frame looked gorgeous as usual. She smiled. "Good morning, Chase."

He looked up and gave her a wide grin. "Good morning, Your Ladyship."

"What are you doing here, Brand?"

"Getting the horses ready for their exercise. Got your horse saddled and ready, ma'am."

His deep, seductive voice sent coils of longing twisting through her stomach. "Thank you, Chase."

"I could have saddled her horse," a testy-sounding Steve countered.

"Just obeyin' Mr. Ted's orders. Your grandpappy told me he wanted Sweet Damsel for her ladyship. Just making sure she got the right horse. He wants to see you by the way."

"What for?"

"Beats me. I don't ask him his business."

"I was going to saddle Lightning."

Chase blew his top. "Lightning! What in thunder were you going to put her on him for? That horse ain't broke enough for a fine lady to ride." Chase's voice rose an octave or two as he spoke.

"I'd watch that tongue of yours, if I were you, Brand. You're getting a mite too cocky for your own good."

"Funny. That's what your grandpappy said about you."

The veins in Steve's neck stood out. He clenched and balled his fist as though he were ready to hit Chase. This was heating up. Best she defuse the situation and do it quickly. She was sure Chase could handle himself, but he wasn't the boss. Come to think of it, neither was Steve. Maybe it would be best if she remove the sexy wrangler from Steve's immediate vicinity before he punched him on the nose. She'd hate to be the cause of an international incident.

"Are we going, Chase? I'd like a decent ride this morning."

Her words stopped him in his tracks. "Sure thing, ma'am." The soft, sexy tone sent shockwaves through her belly. Goodness, that voice could make any woman forget she was a lady.

When Steve had gone, Chase led the way out of the yard, along the bridle path to the fields beyond, and she nudged her horse alongside him.

"Sorry about what happened at the stable. Not a nice thing for guests to see."

"He, uh, he said you'd quit, and that you were packing."

"Quit? I didn't quit. He fired me." They urged their horses up a steep slope. "Seeing as he ain't the boss, I went to see Ted, find out what gives. I don't like the idea of quitting on a guest halfway through a week. He blew his top. Not at me, at Steve."

"I must say I'm happy about that."

"He been giving you trouble? I notice he said no more about you being his girl."

"Let's not talk about him. So, tell me, are we still going to the Covered Wagon café? I really enjoyed that last week."

"Sure are. Now, let's enjoy our ride."

****

Chase looked at the sky. "Dammit. Would you look at those clouds rolling in?"

"Where did they come from?"

"Better try to make it back before the heavens open."

She laughed. "Race you back."

Chase let out the sexiest chuckle she'd ever heard. "Come on then." He urged his horse into a full gallop.

They had only been racing for a few moments before Sweet Damsel stumbled, throwing Laura to the ground. "Chase!"

When he saw what had happened, he turned his horse around and was at her side in an instant. "Laura. Are you all right?"

She brushed grass from her front. "Yes. I'm okay.

What about the horse?"

"I'll take a look." He ran his hands over Sweet Damsel's legs and blew out a breath of relief. "No bones broken, but her right fore is very tender. You won't be able to ride her."

She glanced at the sky. "We won't make it back before the rain hits, either."

He looked around. "We'll head for that stand of trees." He mounted his horse and offered his hand. "Here, swing up behind me."

"You go on. I'll walk with Sweet Damsel. We'll catch you up."

"And leave you here? No chance. Now get up here behind me. If we get wet, we get wet together. We'd better head for those trees."

Laura climbed up behind him and placed her arms around his waist. It was slow going leading a lame horse, but Laura didn't mind. Unable to stop herself, she rested her cheek against his back. He felt so good. Warm and solid.

The rain started, slowly at first, but they managed to reach the stand of trees just as the heavens opened. Laura dismounted, followed by Chase. "Looks dry over there."

He unpacked a blanket from his saddle bag and laid it on the dry earth. "Here you go. I'll call in and let them know where we are," he said, and pulled a cell phone from his jacket pocket.

"Is that absolutely necessary?"

He looked at her under the brim of his Stetson. "Not if you don't want me to."

She sat and patted the blanket.

Chase stretched out beside her. "So, you looking forward to going home?"

"Not particularly. I'd rather stay here."

"What? You'd swap all you have in England, for this?"

"Like a shot. I've always been in love with the West, as you know. Besides, people are more important to me than all my so-called privileges."

He glanced at her. "Any people in particular?"

"You."

"Me?"

"Will you kiss me, Chase?"

"We're not supposed to get involved with the guests."

"Does that mean you don't want to kiss me?"

He smiled. "Heck, no. I've been aching to kiss you since I met you at the airport."

She slipped her arms around his neck. "So, what's stopping you?"

"Why, nothing at all. Be my pleasure, ma'am." He leaned into her. "It ain't every cowboy can say he kissed a real lady."

"And that she kissed him back."

He pulled her into his firm body, and the moment their lips touched, her heart soared. Oh, he felt good, she just had to grip him tighter.

"Do you want to stay here in the States? With me?"

"I'd love to. What are my chances?"

"Oh, I'd say they were food, Real good." And he kissed her again.

The Heart Necklace

by

Amanda Uhl

"You sold it? You sold my painting?"

Olivia looked left, then right, peering at the walls and shelves in the Cleveland thrift shop, as if by some miracle she might spy the precious vintage painting hidden underneath the clutter of household items, furniture, toys and clothes. Her horrified gaze moved past an antique wagon and a portrait of a woman skiing in nineteenth-century garb and landed on the shop owner, a short stocky woman with no makeup and graying hair pulled into a bun.

The woman grimaced. "I am so sorry, my dear. I hung it in the window, and a bunch of customers came in right after you dropped off the item. You said you wanted to sell, and I could set the price, so I did."

"I didn't mean to sell *that* painting. I gave you the wrong one." Tears rushed to Olivia's eyes, and she blinked to stop them from spilling over.

The woman crossed her arms and flashed an anxious look, as if worried Olivia accused her of stealing the artwork.

Olivia swallowed, and her voice trembled. "It's not your fault. It was my mistake. The painting you sold was supposed to go to a frame shop to repair the backing that's torn. This is the painting I meant to sell." She handed the shop owner another framed painting.

"Oh my. Was the painting I sold very valuable then?"

Olivia clutched the counter and took a breath to calm

her nerves. Getting emotional wouldn't help her recover the artwork. "It isn't valuable. Not really. I mean, it was appraised for two hundred dollars, so it has some value, but it was more a cherished family heirloom. The couple in the portrait were my grandparents. It was painted in the 1920s on the day they got engaged."

Olivia fingered the antique gold heart locket around her neck. Grandma Eileen had been wearing the locket when the portrait was painted. She claimed the necklace brought true love to the wearer. It was inscribed with the words "Your Heart for Keeps," and the clasped hands in the center encircled a sparkling red ruby. She'd given it to Olivia's mother. It had certainly worked for her parents who had a wonderful marriage up until their deaths. Her mother had given the necklace to Olivia on her deathbed. "Wear it always," she had said. She'd placed it around her daughter's neck, and there it had stayed. Olivia had only taken it off to shower.

The shop owner scratched her head and watched Olivia like she thought she might faint. "Well, I sold the painting to a gentleman. He bought it for fifty dollars."

"Do you have any idea who he is?"

"No, I don't. He left as fast as he arrived. About all I remember is he had dark hair. Youngish. Quite tall. He seemed to really like the portrait. I heard him say, 'Remarkable.' "

"Is there a way to contact him?"

"Not that I'm aware of—I don't have an address, and he paid cash."

Olivia's eyes burned, and she blinked to stop the tears from rolling down her face. The past year had been the saddest of her entire twenty-four years. Her adored father had died of kidney failure in June and her beloved mother of lung cancer over Thanksgiving. Olivia had been numbed by their deaths so close together; she barely remembered Christmas.

She busied herself rummaging in her purse for a card. She was all alone, except for the painting, the locket, her parents' house on Park Street, and Smudges, her parents' cat. And now, she'd lost the painting. A symbol of her family's everlasting love gone—vanished into a stranger's hands like her parents' lives had been snuffed out. Her fingers trembled, and she fought to steady them. Losing the painting was like losing her beloved parents all over again.

She handed the business card to the store owner. "If the man should happen to stop by again or you remember anything, anything at all, please call me at the phone number on this card. Please. I will pay anything to get the painting back."

The woman studied the card and nodded her head. "If he stops in again, I'll let you know."

There was nothing to be done then except leave the shop and head to her parents' house, where she had piles and piles of boxes to rummage through and dressers and closets full of her parents' belongings. As an only child, the job of clearing her parents' house of their possessions fell on her. Her stomach gurgled, as if in rebellion.

She took a deep breath and started the car, driving the few miles until she arrived at the house, which was now hers. If she hadn't been so overwhelmed with grief, she never would have placed the painting into the trunk with the other painting she'd dropped off at the thrift store this morning, which was how she'd gotten the two confused.

She bit her lip and tasted salty tears. She swiped at

her watery eyes. Who knew if she'd ever see the painting again?

She parked the car and stared at the brick bungalow where she'd taken her first baby steps. If she listened hard enough, she could almost hear her mother's warm laugh, getting ready for a fancy party, the gold heart sparkling around her neck. "Oh, Daniel, you know you have my heart for keeps," her mother would say before her parents left the house, their arms wrapped around one another. And her father's deep baritone would answer, "And what a precious heart it is."

Her mother and father's voices faded from Olivia's memory, and she returned to the present and the gray February day—Valentine's Day. Her mother gone. Her father gone. There was no one left to celebrate this day of love with her—to remember her first birthday, her first day of kindergarten, her first date. No one to walk her down the aisle one day or to be grandparents to her future children. No painting to remind her of her family's legacy. No true love for Olivia like her parents and grandparents had experienced.

A driver passed by, laying on the horn and shaking Olivia from her morbid thoughts. She let out a breath and opened the car door. Dwelling on her parents' deaths wouldn't help her get the house in order. Besides, all was not lost. She still had the necklace and Smudges.

"Meow, meow."

Smudges pushed against her ankles the moment Olivia opened the side door and stepped inside. Poor Smudges. He was as lonely for her parents as Olivia.

"Hey, there, Kitty," she said, stroking his glossy black and white fur. "Let's get you something to eat."

Smudges followed her into the kitchen. Olivia

sniffed the air. She could almost smell the pancakes her mother always whipped up on Sundays. She found the plastic container of cat food and bent over to pour the nuggets into his dish. A flash of gold caught her attention from where the heart necklace dangled from her neck.

The chain was broken.

Panic surged through her veins as she stood and pulled the chain from around her neck. Where was the locket? Had she lost it?

She searched her clothing first, and when it didn't turn up there, the floor in the kitchen and dining room, her heart pumping furiously all the while. The locket was nowhere to be found. Vanished who knew where. Vanished as surely as the painting. Vanished like her parents never to return again.

A sob tore from her throat, and she slid in a heap to the dining room floor, ducking her head into her knees and wrapping her arms around them. Smudges rubbed against her legs, mewing. Shudders racked her body. Why had she been so careless? She'd hardly looked at the necklace this morning when she'd put it on after her shower. Her mind had been preoccupied with her to-do list. And now the locket was gone forever.

Olivia lifted her head to look at the broken chain still fisted in her hand. She would retrace her steps. She'd had the locket earlier at the thrift store. Maybe it was outside in the driveway. Or maybe she'd find it inside the store.

She jumped to her feet and raced to the car. She peered at the ground for a glint of gold or red, but there was nothing but stones and dirt. She searched the car seats and the floor, lifting up the mats and digging into the crevices. *Nothing.* Heart pounding, she raced to the house to fetch her purse and keys.

Then she was back in the car and tearing down the street, heading to the thrift store. When she arrived, panicked and out of breath, she tore into the shop to confront the store owner, who came from behind the counter, eyes wide.

"What is it, dear? Have you recovered the painting?"

"No, I lost the heart from my necklace. Have you found it?" Olivia didn't wait for an answer but swept the floor with her eyes, hoping to spy a glimmer of gold.

The woman shook her head sadly. "No, I'm sorry. I haven't found anything. You're welcome to stay and look around for it, though."

And Olivia did. But an hour later, she returned to her car empty-handed and dejected. She had searched every nook and cranny in the small store and walked to and from her car dozens of times, hoping to spy the missing piece. She received nothing but dust balls and rocks for her trouble.

Panic settled into a hard ball in her chest. She clutched her stomach, which dropped like the bottom of an elevator attraction she'd once ridden at a local amusement park. The ride had eventually stopped, and she'd gotten off. But today, the ride seemed endless. An endless journey with loneliness and despair her only companions.

She climbed into her car and tipped her head back against the seat cushion. She hadn't thought there were tears left to cry, but they came anyway, pouring forth from an endless cavern inside her heart. First the painting, now her cherished locket. Was she to be stripped of everything she once held dear? *Oh Lord, why can't this sorrow end? Saint Valentine, if you're listening, can you send a little love my way? Mom, Dad,*

I miss you so much. If you can hear me, please help me find the locket.

****

Liam Reilly clasped his hands together and studied the gold piece in front of him. Sometimes, even he was unsure what shape would take place under his fingertips. A vague thought would form, maybe from a dream, maybe from a slice of life, and it might inspire his next masterpiece or it might not. Usually, what he made sold and sold fast. But sometimes it became part of his permanent collection—an item so unusual the right buyer couldn't be found, and the piece had to be removed for a more sellable one.

A shape began to form in the soft gold. Satisfaction bloomed in his gut. It appeared today's effort would produce a sellable piece.

Liam had appreciated art since he was a small child. But he had no talent for painting or pottery. His medium was jewelry, which is why, at the urging of his best friend, Sean, he'd left his job as a welder and put his creative talents to use at Skilled Expressions, his and Sean's jewelry store. Despite their passion for the business, they'd only begun to turn a profit this Christmas.

The phone rang, and Sean took the call. He could hear his partner haggling over the price. Yes, he could probably have it repaired today. Yes, the shop employed a skilled craftsman who would carefully consider the age of the piece. Yes, they insured their work and their customer's satisfaction. Sean hung up and came to the back of the store where Liam worked.

"Did you hear that? Another job. A lady needs her antique chain repaired. She seemed upset. Said the chain broke, and she wanted it fixed right away before she lost it. I told her you would take a look, and if anyone could repair it in a day, it would be you. Am I a liar? I hate to turn away paying customers."

Liam smiled. "You didn't lie."

"I told you this business would turn a profit sooner than either you or I expected."

Liam's smile widened at his friend's enthusiasm. "And you'll never let me forget it."

Sean grinned. "Listen, I gotta leave, or Marie will have a panic attack. Tonight's parent-teacher conference, and you know, Patrick's grades haven't been good. You okay? The customer is on her way in now."

Liam nodded. "Don't worry. I'll take care of her."

"All right then, I'm outta here. See you tomorrow." Sean walked towards the door, but turned with a smile. "Now, aren't you glad you're here doing what you love?"

Liam laughed. "Night, Sean."

"Night, buddy."

After Sean left the shop, Liam continued working. There was something almost spiritual about the piece in front of him. It seemed to take shape without effort. The clock ticked on in the small room where he labored, but all other sounds faded from existence. So engrossed was he in the job, he didn't look up until he'd finished the final touches and set his tools down to admire his handiwork.

The jangle of the bell over the door erupted, breaking the stillness. He left his work to see who had entered. The customer had her back to him, studying the jewelry in the case, so he didn't immediately see her face until she turned. Her eyes struck him first—as rich a blue as the cobalt glass he sometimes collected. They glittered finer than starlight on the ocean. His heart hiccuped in his chest before resuming a steady, faster beat.

She hesitated, smoothing a hand across her forehead then tucking it into her coat pocket. "Hello. I called earlier about my broken chain. You said you could repair it today."

Her hair was the next thing he noticed—vibrant red and straight, a startling contrast to her white skin. And she smelled like cinnamon and vanilla and the sand on the shore of his favorite Lake Erie beach.

He cleared his throat. "That was Sean you spoke with. My business partner. I'm Liam Reilly. I'll have to take a look. I may be able to fix it. A lot depends on where it broke." He forced his gaze past her eyes and swollen red lips to settle on her long fingers, which clutched a small, square box she pulled from her pocket.

She held it out to him almost tenderly. "Nice to meet you, Liam. I'm Olivia Manning. This necklace is very old and very dear." Her voice hitched. "I've only got the chain now. I lost the heart locket today that went with it."

Liam studied her trembling hands as he took the case and opened it, his own hands not quite steady either. He pulled the glittery antique chain from the box and held it up to the light.

"What's the matter? Can you not repair it?"

Her worried gaze met his, and his tongue stuck to the roof of his mouth. He couldn't very well say her beauty had turned his brain to mush, could he? He managed a smile. "No, it should be an easy fix. I just need to grab a tool from my workbench. How old is the chain?"

She followed him to the back and watched as he

made the repair. "It was my mother's, and before hers, my grandmother's."

"It's a beautiful chain." He made a few more adjustments with his tool and showed her the necklace. "Here, returned to its former glory."

Olivia gasped, but she was not looking at the chain. No, she looked over his shoulder.

He turned to see what had alarmed her. She was gazing in astonishment at his work in progress.

****

Olivia moved towards the piece of gold laying on a cloth on the work table afraid to blink, afraid to hope, afraid to dream. "Where…where did you get this?"

Liam came behind her. She could smell the musky scent of his cologne. It did strange things to her insides. She didn't need to look at him. She knew what she'd see. Liam was quite good-looking with his dark curly hair and strong chin. His brown eyes seemed to see more than she wanted to share.

He reached her side. "You like it?" He smiled when she looked his way, offering her a tantalizing glimpse of straight, white teeth. His deep voice fit his dark, good looks.

She found herself leaning towards him, mesmerized. "I love it."

"I made it." A dimple appeared in one stubbled cheek and vanished. "It's not finished. I still need to add…"

She cleared her throat. "A ruby in its center."

Liam cocked his head to the side and shot her a puzzled look. "That's right. How did you know?"

"This is my locket. The one that hung from my chain up until this afternoon."

"Your locket." His gaze narrowed and his brow furrowed.

Olivia's heartbeat, which had finally evened to a steady cadence, galloped again. "Yes, the one I said I lost earlier. You must have found it…"

Liam held up a hand. "I didn't find it. I made it."

"You made it? But how?" She reached out and touched the heart, which felt cool on her fingertips. "It's perfect. Tell the truth. Were you outside the thrift store on Vine Street today? Did you find my locket in the parking lot?"

Liam's expression went from puzzlement to understanding. He smiled. "I think you need to come with me. I believe I have something that will interest you."

She followed Liam into a side room. A painting hung on the wall. She stopped moving in mid-stride. The room spun madly, and she would have collapsed in a puddle at his feet if he didn't grab her hand and hold her up.

"You…you bought the painting from the thrift store."

It was a statement and not a question, but he answered as if it was the most important question in the universe. "I did. I couldn't stop looking at it. There is such love shining from the subject's fine eyes. And now I think I see the connection. But that's not what convinced me to buy the painting."

"What then?"

"It was the locket. The clasped hands are unbreakable, aren't they? Almost as one unit rather than two separate parts. And the glittering ruby. I feel it emphasizes the couple's love and the continual nature of their partnership. The necklace is a masterpiece. I couldn't resist trying to emulate it."

"That's amazing," she said, but she knew she was talking about much more than the locket.

"Here." He smiled, setting the chain back in its box and lifting the painting to offer it to her. "I cannot keep this, knowing it belongs to you."

"Thank you," she said, taking the painting from his hands. Joy rose in her chest like a helium balloon. "I hadn't meant to sell it and am so happy to have it returned." There was something marvelous about this man, Liam, and it was not just his good looks. It was as if he could read her soul—all the loneliness and despair she'd kept locked away—and was not shocked or embarrassed by the feelings. Instead, she felt sympathy in his gaze and something more. Something she couldn't quite name. Something which nearly had her melting into his arms.

"Well," she said, when the silence between them stretched a moment too long. "Thank you for returning the painting to me."

"It's my pleasure. There's a coffee shop next door. May I buy you a cup of coffee or tea?"

Olivia nodded. She didn't know quite what was happening, but she wasn't fool enough to walk away from whatever it was.

"Just give me a minute to finish up. You can put the painting in your car so you don't have to carry it. I'll meet you out front and bring the necklace."

She did as he suggested and ten minutes later, he met her at her car and handed her the box with her necklace, which she deposited on the front seat. They walked together towards the shop next door.

"Do you live in the area?" he asked.

"Yes, I have a house not far from here. What about you?"

"I live here." He laughed and pointed at the jewelry store. "There are rooms upstairs."

They made their way to the coffee shop and placed their orders, and soon they were chatting like old friends and not new acquaintances. He told her about his love of art and decision to risk everything and open the store. She described her struggle to overcome her parents' deaths. And somewhere in their conversation, a strange thing happened. Two people connected in something larger than themselves. A circle of life perhaps or maybe love. A Valentine's Day miracle.

Olivia set her cup down. Her coffee had long since grown cold. And although she didn't really want to leave Liam, she knew it was time to say goodnight.

"May I see you again?" he asked.

She smiled. "I'd like that."

They exchanged numbers, and he walked her to her car. She drove home as if in a dream, the painting in the trunk and the chain in its box on the seat next to her.

It wasn't until much later, after dinner had been eaten and Smudges appeared briefly and was fed, that she thought to take a look at the chain. She opened up the square box and studied the necklace a moment in the warm kitchen light.

Her hands shook as she pulled it from its box. She fought a rush of hot tears. But these were not the tears of despair from this afternoon. No, these were tears of happiness and hope. For inside the case was a note that read simply, "For my Valentine."

She picked up the necklace and gazed at it in

wonder. Hanging from the chain was a shiny golden heart with a red ruby at its center. Two beautiful hands grasped one another in a timeless bond. It was the locket Liam had made. He must have added the ruby and slipped it inside the case before he returned it to her.

Saint Valentine was blessed with gifts of love and faith. A faith so strong he was jailed and put to death. A love so powerful he miraculously restored a blind girl's sight. He gifted the world with Valentine's Day—a day of love. Some might call the return of the painting and locket a coincidence. Some might call it a lucky break.

But as she gazed at the heart necklace and thought of its maker, Olivia knew the truth. The locket had brought her true love.

"Thanks, Mom and Dad," she whispered, fastening the necklace around her neck. "And thank you, Saint Valentine."

Author's Note:

Saint Valentine, the patron saint of Valentine's Day, was beheaded by Emperor Claudius the second in AD270. Claudius thought married men made poor soldiers, so he banned marriage from his empire. But Valentine secretly married young couples that came to him. For this, Valentine was imprisoned, tortured, and eventually, stoned and beheaded. During the days Valentine was imprisoned, he befriended his jailer's blind daughter. Legend has it that because of his love for her, and his great faith, he miraculously was able to heal her from her blindness before his death. Before he died, he signed a farewell message to her, "From your Valentine." The phrase has been used on Valentine's Day ever since.

The Relaxation Response

by

Darcy Lundeen

J. Markley Mathews walked briskly down the corridor to her apartment. The heels of her expensive shoes clicked rhythmically on the polished floor. The skirt of her fashionable business suit swirled beguilingly around her slender hips. The curls of her stylish hairdo swung gently against her delicate cheeks.

J. Markley Mathews looked exactly the way she was supposed to look—like a young bottom-rung account executive confidently on her way up the slippery ladder of career success.

Back home in Kentucky, no one would have recognized her. Of course, back home in Kentucky, J. Markley Mathews didn't exist. There, she was known to most people simply as Jane Mathews, and to her immediate family and very close friends, even more simply as Janie.

But since she'd moved to New York four months ago, almost everything about her had changed. She'd assumed a completely different persona. Her clothes had gone from simple to sleek, her makeup from passable to perfect, her outward manner from small-town friendly to big-city cool and cautious. And deep down…well, deep down, the metamorphosis wasn't yet complete, and perhaps it never would be. Deep down, she was still Janie Mathews.

But some of her new coworkers, helpful to a fault, had taken her under their wing and solemnly informed her that being Janie Mathews—a sweet, open, vaguely naïve girl from out West—wouldn't be enough to allow her to survive and flourish in the big city. She needed something more than that—a poise and polish she just didn't have. So, she had developed them. She had taken on a whole new self.

And to tell the absolute truth, she hated it.

She also wasn't too thrilled about most of the men she'd met so far. They were too suave and knowing, when all she wanted was a down-home kind of guy she could relax with.

Footsteps—long, striding, no-nonsense footsteps—suddenly echoed behind Janie, and she turned to look at the man who had just gotten off the elevator. The briefcase in his hand told her he was probably coming home from work, and the cut of his well-made suit, plus the self-assured movement of his body told her he was like too many of the men she had already met—suave and knowing.

What a shame. Her shoulders drooped. He was such a nice-looking man, too. She bit back a sigh and opened her front door as the man strode past her to an apartment down the hall.

Once inside her living room, she discarded the persona of J. Markley Mathews just as quickly and completely as she discarded her fashionable clothes, tossing her tote bag and jacket aside and kicking off her shoes with a groan of relief.

Then she padded in her stockinged feet over to the large aquarium in the corner and looked down at her sleek and slippery roommates.

Tapping gently at the side of the tank, she bent closer so that she could greet them as she watched their aquatic hijinks. "Hello, Zig…hello, Zag."

The two goldfish seemed to be playing a game of tag around the castle and the helmeted figure of a deep-sea diver that were nestled at the bottom of the tank. Sometimes she talked to them as though they were old friends. It relaxed her. Besides, in a way they *were* old friends, or the closest thing she could find to old friends here in her new home. Anyone who didn't care that she was just Janie Mathews was, in her opinion, an old friend. And these fish definitely didn't care.

Picking up a container of fish-food flakes, she shook some into the water as she launched into the rundown she always gave them on how her day had been. "Today, I gave Mr. Saunders the report I did on the McCready account. He said it was very good."

The goldfish scrambled for the food, circling each other as they swam. Zig, the one with the bright orange sheen to his skin, looped around the helmeted diver to catch the sinking flakes in his ravenous mouth, while Zag, the silvery one with the beautifully long, flowy tail, burrowed among the stones at the bottom of the tank, searching for his meal there.

Janie gave the box another shake. She enjoyed feeding the fish, especially when she was feeling anxious or lonely. It relaxed her, just the way that talking to them did.

"Samantha also invited me to a party at her house on Saturday. I told her I'd go." She couldn't help frowning. She didn't really want to attend Samantha's party because she already knew the kind of people who would be there—cool, brittle, wonderfully sophisticated big-city people. But she also didn't want to be rude to a co-worker, especially one like Samantha, who had done so much to help her put together her new image. In the end, against her better judgment, she had agreed to go.

"I wonder what I should wear," she said to the fish.

They were too busy eating to even give the appearance of being interested, so Janie put down the container of food and padded into the bathroom.

Her face in the medicine-cabinet mirror surprised her, as it often did these days. Except for the slightly too-generous mouth and the slightly too-deep-set large blue eyes, every feature seemed smooth, silky, and beautifully shaded. Almost flawless, in fact. In short, completely unlike the real her.

She lathered her hands with soap and rubbed them vigorously over her face, wiping away the perfect canvas of makeup. Suddenly the old Janie began to emerge, all fresh-cheeked innocence, with a vague smattering of decidedly unsophisticated freckles across her nose.

That's better. She rumpled her hair into a mass of flyaway curls to complete the transformation.

She was just turning away from the mirror when she glanced down and noticed the pipes under the sink. One of them seemed to be glistening. Janie bent to examine it, letting her hand glide along the slightly damp surface.

"Lord, I hope it's not a leak," she murmured.

But there was only a fine mist of water gilding the pipe, and after a moment she sighed with relief. *No, no leak, nothing serious.* The pipe was probably just sweating.

She straightened, brushing a hand across her cheek to push the hair out of her eyes, and caught a glimpse of herself in the mirror. There was a smudge of dirt from the pipe on her face. She grinned, and the smudge widened, spreading across her cheek.

What would Samantha's sophisticated friends think

if they could see her now, all dirty, disheveled, and blissfully comfortable? Hmm, what about the man who'd passed her in the hall? What in the world would that man—that tall, attractive, undeniably elegant man—think if he could see her now?

****

The next day, when she was coming home from work, Janie saw him again. To be more accurate, he saw Janie, and fortunately for her, just in time, or else the closing elevator doors would have come close to crushing her.

She had just entered the lobby of the apartment building when she noticed that the elevator was standing there, its doors wide open and seemingly beckoning to her. She immediately headed for it, her expensive shoes clicking, the skirt of her fashionable business suit swirling.

As she ran toward the open doors, she didn't see him standing in a corner of the elevator. Luckily, he saw her, and when the doors started to close, almost catching her between them, he pressed the "open" button, then quickly grabbed one door to force it back.

Janie managed to stumble into the enclosure with her body intact, her hair and clothing slightly askew, and her poise totally demolished.

"Uh, thank you." Straightening her jacket and hitching her tote bag higher on her shoulder, she moved to a corner of the elevator across from where he stood and desperately tried to regain her composure without looking like she'd ever lost it.

He narrowed his eyes at her as though he didn't for a minute believe that she was the perfect picture of self-assured serenity.

"Are you all right?"

She tried surreptitiously to smooth back her disheveled hair. Then in order to reassure him that she was just fine, *thank you very much*, she deliberately flashed a smile. "Oh, yes. Yes, I'm fine. Totally perfect."

As the elevator began to move, she reached out to press the eighth-floor button, stopping abruptly when she realized that since they lived on the same floor, he had already pressed it.

"You're on eight, too?" he asked.

Janie nodded, trying not to look too interested as she took a quick mental inventory of the man. He had a nice deep voice and nice dark eyes and he was tall and vaguely athletic looking. She noticed his clothes, too. *Expensive*. And his briefcase. *Probably genuine leather, and very expensive*. Obviously, the man was just as successful as she assumed, and undoubtedly just as unapproachable too.

"Oh, that's right."

He inclined his head to her, then his gaze raked over her in a slow, appraising way. Whoa, he was studying her as hard as she had been studying him.

"I recognize you now. You moved in pretty recently, didn't you?"

"Yes. About four months ago."

He nodded and smiled at her. A nice smile, but not quite as friendly and hello-neighbor effusive as the smiles of the guys back home.

"Well, welcome to the building. I'm Glenn Spencer. Nice to meet you."

He extended his hand in a gesture that seemed automatic—the thing businessmen tended to do when they met people at formal receptions and wanted to make a good impression.

Janie smiled and took his hand. It was large and warm, with one of those firm, no-nonsense handshakes she always associated with successful men intent on showing the world exactly how in control they were.

"Nice to meet you too, I'm…" For a minute, she was awfully tempted to tell him the truth—that her name was Janie Mathews, just plain Janie Mathews. But thinking about his upscale clothes and that really impressive, pricy briefcase of his, she stopped herself in time and instead ticked off the new, city persona she'd created. "I'm J. Markley Mathews."

"J? You mean…J-A-Y?"

"No, just the initial J."

"Oh. J. Markley Mathews."

She disentangled her hand from his. His tone implied that he considered the name unusual, if not downright strange. She began to feel a little defensive about it. After all, men often used their first initial and nobody gave it a second thought…so why shouldn't she?

"Yes, Mr. Spencer." She deliberately firmed her voice, trying to sound decisive, but not obnoxiously so. "J. Markley Mathews."

The elevator lurched to a stop, putting a merciful end to the conversation, and he let her get out first, then followed as he nodded politely to her.

"Well, good night."

"Good night." Janie stopped before her door.

As she fished in her bag for her key, she cautiously watched him from the corner of her eye to see where he went. He paused at an apartment four doors away. Ah. That was where he lived. Apartment 8-E.

Janie entered her foyer and closed the door behind

her. Down the hall, his door closed, too. She shook her head with regret. What a shame he was like so many of the other rising young executive-types she'd met, all smooth lines and polished surfaces.

For a moment, the possibility crossed her mind that perhaps she might be wrong, perhaps he might somehow be different underneath, maybe a little less sophisticated and secure than he seemed.

"After all, you can't always judge a book by its cover," she intoned softly as she kicked off her shoes and hurried into the living room to describe the latest, totally boring events of the day to her two fishy confidants.

But it was just a passing thought, and in the case of people like Glenn Spencer, she wasn't really sure that she believed it. So she forced the subject from her mind, because right now she had more important things to consider. Samantha's party was tomorrow, and she had to decide what to wear and how to do her hair.

She would probably have to look as sleek as possible for the occasion. That meant her hair done up in a chignon and her body encased in that gorgeous blue dress she'd recently bought. It was the most sophisticated thing she owned, and she had the unnerving feeling that this party was going to be nothing if not sophisticated.

****

As soon as she reached Samantha's party, Janie knew she had been right. The apartment was beautifully decorated; the food was luscious beyond belief; and the people were well-dressed, well-read, well-traveled, and just a little too intimidating for her taste.

She snuck a glance at her cell phone to check the time. Eight o'clock. She had been here for nearly ninety minutes, and during that brief interval one guest had told her more than she cared to know about his job as an up-and-coming corporate attorney, while another guest had described in glowing detail her most recent one-woman show at an exclusive downtown art gallery. In response, Janie had been sorely tempted to tell them about the terrific McCready report she'd done for Mr. Saunders but, luckily, shyness and an unerring sense of caution had stopped her before she could make a total fool of herself.

She wandered over to the buffet table for the third time that evening. Not because she was hungry, but just for something to do so that she wouldn't have to talk to anyone and reveal that she was only a very small minnow in a very large pond.

She perused the sumptuous spread, then spooned some shrimp and asparagus tips onto her plate and began to eat. It was good. No. Better than good. Absolutely delicious. But what she really wanted was a pizza swimming in tomato sauce and melted cheese and piled high with mushrooms and nice spicy pepperoni.

"Last summer, when I was in Paris, there was the most fabulous exhibit at the Louvre."

The woman standing next to her was conversing with a young man.

"I didn't go to Europe last summer," he replied. "Just up to my place in the Hamptons. But at Christmas I did take a week off for this unbelievable photographic safari in East Africa. I must show you the pictures sometime."

Very quietly, Janie put her plate down and went to find Samantha to tell her good night. It was best to leave now, before someone asked what she had done on *her* summer vacation, and she was forced to admit she had spent it in Kentucky, helping her dad paint the house.

****

When she got home, she gratefully took off her beautiful dress and changed into jeans, sneakers, and an oversized shirt.

"The party was a little intimidating, guys. Really it was," she told Zig and Zag a few minutes later as she sprinkled food into their tank. "All these confident people with wonderful jobs and exotic vacations."

By then the fish were at the bottom of the tank, too busy eating to pay any attention to her. Janie sighed and checked the mantel clock. It was only nine fifteen. She would wash her face, make a cup of tea, and watch TV until bedtime. Not a very exciting way to spend a Saturday night, but after Samantha's party, it was exactly what she wanted.

She went into the bathroom and scrubbed the makeup from her face. Then she took down her carefully styled hair and let it go flyaway, the way she usually wore it when she was at home in Kentucky.

She reached out to turn off the light and go into the kitchen. Uh-oh, the floor by the sink was damp. Just the splash-over of water from the basin, right? She bent down to check more closely. Crud. No, it wasn't.

Frowning, she ran her hand along one of the pipes. Oh, no. What she had thought was sweating the other day wasn't sweating at all. It was an honest-to-goodness leak. She finally found the source—the fitting between two pipes. Water was oozing out of it, and Janie got to her knees, wondering what to do.

She didn't know anything about plumbing, but maybe if she fiddled with those two ends a bit, she might be able to stem the flow. So, foolishly, she fiddled, and that was when disaster struck. Instead of coaxing the seams together, she somehow managed to force them farther apart, and the water began to flow more freely. Not gushing, exactly, but dripping with a speed that seemed almost ominous.

This was no job for a home-repairs incompetent like her. She ran into the living room to call for help.

First, she speed-dialed the super's number, but no one answered. Down in Mr. Bollinger's ground-floor apartment, the phone simply blared on and on, its steady buzz echoing in her ear.

After a few seconds, Janie ended the call in exasperation, then immediately tapped in the management office's number. Who would be there at nine twenty on a Saturday night?

Nobody.

Just a recorded message informing her that the office was closed and wouldn't reopen until Monday morning at eight thirty.

"At the sound of the beep," the message ordered, "leave your name, number, and the reason for your call, and someone will get back to you as soon as possible."

Not soon enough to keep my apartment from becoming a swimming pool.

But she left the requested information anyway, then accessed a search engine so that she could look up nearby plumbers. By the time she called several of them and butted heads with a collection of Saturday-night, We're-not-here-but-we'll-get-back-to-you-as-soon-as-possible recordings that bore an eerie similarity to the management office's message, her mood was bordering on hysteria.

Gritting her teeth in frustration, Janie tossed the cell on an end table and ran into the bathroom to check the progress of the leak. The puddle seemed to be spreading rapidly. One outflung finger of water had already reached the corner of the tub. She wiped it with a towel, then turned her attention to mopping up the puddle under the sink as more water seeped onto her hands from the broken pipe.

Janie pushed a lock of hair out of her eyes and groaned as she stared helplessly at the developing disaster. Back home, every neighbor she had would have been over in three seconds to help. But this wasn't back home. This was the big city. And even after four months, she still didn't know any of her neighbors. Except for that man in—*where was it?*—8-E.

But he hardly seemed like the type to be overly helpful, especially in a plumbing emergency. He was much too suave-looking and sophisticated. Still, there was nothing else that she could think of to do. She pulled another towel from the rack and dried her hands on it, then wrapped it around the pipe to temporarily stem the leak.

She didn't even glance at herself in the foyer mirror as she left the apartment. She didn't have the nerve. Besides, she already knew what she looked like—her hair was flying around her face, her complexion was shiny from lack of makeup, and her faded jeans and loose shirttails were casual to the point of sloppiness. For the moment, J. Markley Mathews was dead, and in her place stood the good-natured, incompetent, and slightly hayseed Janie Mathews.

She hesitated for an instant outside the man's apartment. Then the thought of the flood developing back in her bathroom galvanized her to desperately ring his bell.

He opened the door almost immediately.

Hey, he was wearing casual clothes, too. In fact, they were nearly the counterpart to her outfit—jeans, sneakers, and a plaid shirt that was pulled out of his waistband and unbuttoned at the throat. But where she looked about twelve years old in her clothes, he still looked sophisticated and knowing in his.

He stared at her with bemusement at first, then recognition suddenly dawned.

"A. Mackey Mason," he said.

"J. Markley Mathews," she corrected. "Mr. Spencer—" She waved frantically toward her own apartment. "—a pipe in my bathroom sprang a leak. I can't stop it, the super isn't home, the management office doesn't open until Monday, and all the plumbers I've called are apparently taking the weekend off. Could you help?"

He paused for a moment, then his face broke into a broad grin and he shrugged. "I'll see what I can do. Lead the way."

****

While he hunkered down in her bathroom, examining the pipe, Janie paced nervously across the living room, praying everything would be all right. She walked over to the aquarium. Zig and Zag were staring at her through the glass, their mouths opening and closing rhythmically as if they were having a fascinating conversation. As she always did when she was anxious, Janie reached for the fish food and sprinkled some into the tank.

Both fish automatically dove for it, polishing off the

flakes like two starving barracuda.

She picked up the container of food again, began to pour some more into the water, then realized what she was doing and put the container down with a sigh. If she kept feeding them this way, pretty soon she'd have the only goldfish in the world that weighed three-hundred pounds each. "Sorry, fellows. I shouldn't be feeding you so much. It's not good for you."

Zig was busily swimming through the little castle at the bottom of the tank, his tail turned toward her. But Zag had returned to Janie's side of the glass and was staring at her as though he was listening. She leaned toward him.

"I hope he can fix that pipe, Zag. If not, this whole place is going to be one gigantic aquarium for you to swim around in."

"No such luck, Zag. No gigantic aquarium. Sorry," Glenn's voice said.

Janie spun around to face him. He was standing in the middle of the room, wiping his hands on a towel and grinning at her. He still looked sophisticated but, somehow, not quite as much as before.

"Do you always talk to your fish?" he asked.

She began to nod, then realized what she was doing and quickly shook her head—*of course not…definitely not*—how could he even think she would engage in such a ridiculous activity? Then for the second time, Janie realized what she was doing and that it was a lie, and she finally gave in. With a shamefaced nod, she admitted the truth.

"Yes, but that's not the worst thing a person can do to relax, you know," she insisted, afraid he might think she was some kind of weirdo. "I mean, I don't do it constantly. I realize they're just fish and that they don't understand what I'm saying."

Glenn came over to the aquarium and tapped on the glass.

Zag was happily busying himself at the far side of the tank, but Zig obligingly swam over and looked at him.

"Hi, Zag," he said.

"Zig," Janie corrected. "The other one's Zag."

"Oh, sorry. Zig." He turned to her. "Zig…Zag. I get it! How'd you come up with those names?"

Janie hesitated. She didn't know if she should tell him. He might laugh at how silly it was. But, then again, he hadn't laughed at how silly she looked, and she looked even sillier than her reason for giving the goldfish their names sounded. Finally, she just blurted it out.

"I noticed that they seem to enjoy swimming around each other, sort of like they're—"

"Zigzagging," he supplied, smiling a little, but definitely not laughing at her. "Very clever. I once had a hamster that I talked to all the time. He finally managed to get out of his cage and run away. I think it was because he got bored listening to my troubles. You're smart to keep fish. At least they can't escape. The most they can do is turn tail on you and swim to the other side of the tank."

Janie couldn't help grinning at that, it was so true. "You're right. That's just what they do to me, turn tail and swim across the aquarium, all the way to the other—" She stopped, suddenly remembering what he'd said before. "Wait a minute. A while ago, you said, no gigantic aquarium. The fish wouldn't have a gigantic aquarium to swim around in. Does that mean that you fixed the pipe?"

"Not quite, but I did turn the cold water valve off to stop the leak."

"You turned the cold water off?"

He nodded. "But you won't have any trouble with the water in the tub and john, so you should be fine until my uncle arrives. I just called him, and he said he can get here from New Jersey in an hour or so. He's a licensed plumber, so he can fix a leak like that in his sleep. And if you really need a bathroom sink in the meantime, just feel free to come to my place and share mine."

Janie stared at him, feeling like a fool. "Oh, I never even thought of just turning off the water." She shrugged with embarrassment. "I'm not too good with things like plumbing and home repairs. Last summer, I helped my father paint the house and ended up with more paint on me than on the walls."

He nodded again. "That's typical of a New Yorker."

"But I'm not from New York. I've just been here a few months. I'm from Kentucky."

"Kentucky?" He grinned. "And what are the natives there good at if not plumbing and home repairs?"

"Oh, horseback riding. I'm terrific with horses."

"Are you? And do you talk to them, too?"

This time, Janie didn't hesitate. She knew that she could tell him and that he wouldn't laugh, except perhaps in a good-natured, nonjudgmental way. "Of course I do. Even more than I talk to fish. I—" She broke off abruptly and stared at him. "Did you say your uncle is a plumber?"

He flashed a smile that told her it was definitely true, and he was pretty proud of it. "Yup. Best damn plumber on the East Coast." Shrugging, he lowered his voice as though he was about to impart a vital secret. "Actually, he's really the best damn plumber in the world, but I don't want to seem like I'm bragging, even though I am. He even tried to teach me when I was a kid. Sadly, I'm the biggest klutz in the whole family. That's why I was forced to go into banking."

For a moment, Janie stared at him in amazement. He used to talk to his hamster, he was the family klutz, and he wore jeans, sneakers, and untucked shirts—the same casual outfit she wore when she was at home.

Suddenly she felt very much at ease and incredibly content, because suddenly Glenn Spencer didn't look all that suave and knowing. He looked…. *Well, exactly how would I phrase it?* But she already knew the words. He looked like the kind of guy that she could relax with, the kind of wonderful guy who had a plumber for an uncle and was damn proud of it.

Taking a breath filled with a sublime, and totally unexpected, sense of relief, she moved a little closer to him. "Mr. Spencer."

"Glenn," he said.

She nodded, happily accepting the correction. "Glenn, would you like something to drink? I mean, since you saved me from drowning in my own living room."

"Love it." He checked the mantel clock. "Not quite ten o'clock. I had supper a few hours ago. I guess you did, too. But if you're willing, I wouldn't mind a small snack right now. Maybe we could call down for some—"

"Pizza." Janie couldn't stop herself from blurting out the word, with a sense of absolute bliss, too. "I've been dying for pizza all evening." She took a breath, realizing that she couldn't help confiding that to him either, because at this point, she was fairly certain he wouldn't mind her almost childlike enthusiasm.

She was right. In answer, he simply smiled, and Janie couldn't help noticing that his smile had suddenly taken on the friendly, hello-neighbor warmth of the guys back home.

"Just what I had in mind," he said. "Pepperoni?"

She nodded. "And mushrooms. Definitely mushrooms. We can save some for your uncle, too, in case he'd like a snack when he gets here."

"Sounds perfect to me. Even the snack for Uncle Danny. Pizza is one of his favorite foods. There's this place down the street. They usually stay open till midnight, and they'll deliver in twenty minutes flat."

He pulled the cell phone out of his pants pocket and was about to tap in a number, when he suddenly paused for a moment to look at her. "By the way, what do I call you? J. or Markley or Ms. Mathews…or what?"

"Jane," she said. "That's what the J. stands for. Jane. Janie Mathews."

"Janie." He said the name slowly as though testing how it felt on his tongue. "You know, Janie, you look different from the last time I saw you. That's why I didn't recognize you when you came to my door."

She ran a hand through her tangled hair, tangling it even more and not caring a bit. "I know. I look terrible. I am, in a word, a total mess."

"Total mess—that's two words," he said, smiling another of his warm, hello-neighbor smiles. "And you don't look terrible at all. Actually, you look very nice. Natural. The kind of woman it's so hard for a man to meet in a town like this."

"Really?" His words so closely mirrored her own

thoughts about men that she couldn't help luxuriating in them as she savored the deliciously mellow feeling that had begun to blossom inside of her. "What kind of woman is that?"

He shrugged, as though searching for the right words. "Oh, you know," he finally said. "Somebody down to earth. Not too sophisticated. The sort of woman a man can just…I don't know…just relax with."

Dancing Through Tears

by

Jeny Heckman

Dedicated to:
The 58 souls murdered
The 869 souls injured
The countless Route 91 survivors and families
whose lives will never be the same as a result of the
Las Vegas attack, October 1, 2017.

Chapter 1
Ginger

Bright blue illuminated the October sky. The sun, its only inhabitant, radiated its warmth and assurance of a glorious start to the month of October in Las Vegas. Ginger Hughes, her family, and their friends spent the day at Top Golf. As they sunbathed, drove golf balls off the top deck, and splashed each other in the pool, they watched their beloved Hawks beat down Indianapolis. It was the first time Ginger and her husband, Jacob, had seen their kids, Faith and Connor, since they left home to go back and start their final year at Eastern Washington University. Connor was finishing a four-year Communications degree, and Faith had stayed on an extra year for her Master's in Business. They came to have fun and attend Route 91, the three-day country music festival, that played in an adjacent arena to their hotel, the Mandalay Bay Resort and Casino.

It was Sunday, the last day of the festival, and the family was leaving early in the morning, on separate planes—the kids, back to their university; her husband, Jake, to a business meeting in Denver; and Ginger back to the comfort of her computer in Northwest Washington State. The Hughes kids and their friends left the fun-plex early, heading back to the family's hotel room to get ready for the concert and begin to pre-funk with cocktails and snacks. Their parents stayed to watch the end of another game before heading back to the hotel themselves.

"You want a shower before we go over there?" Jake asked, indicating the festival.

"I'm not sure if I want to go tonight," Ginger responded absently, as she sipped the last dregs of her beer and set it on the counter. "We won't get back until late, and we have to be to the airport by seven. You saw the room before we left." Thinking of the cramped living space in their small hotel room, she wrinkled her brow. "Imagine what it looks like now." Her husband of twenty-five years grinned back at her.

"Nope, not gonna do it."

She laughed. "Anyway, I thought I'd skip tonight and go pack everyone up. You know they're gonna be wasted when they get back."

"All right," her husband replied, "I'm with you." He kissed her gently before turning to the waiter and the check.

Ginger smiled at his outfit, a gray Hawks jersey and the ugliest bright orange swim shorts she'd ever seen. She sent a text to her offspring about the change of plan before leaning over to pick up the beach bag. She shoved their towels and suntan lotion into it, along with their cellphones and wallets.

"So, you're helping me pack?" she asked in astonishment.

"No, I'll supervise." His eyes widened. "No, I'll go play blackjack. It'll be a lot more fun." He smirked at her, and she answered with an eye roll.

"Fine," she chuckled, before turning to the attendant, "Thank you so much."

"You bet. Enjoy your night."

"You too."

As the couple approached their temporary home via taxicab, they heard the deep bass of the country music. The concert venue was kitty-corner from Mandalay Bay, and hordes of fans weaved between the cars, when the light changed to yellow. Kids in their early twenties, younger, older, male and female, all burst out in a beloved song as they raced toward the venue. Ginger looked through the chain-link fence and knew where the kids would be. It was the same place they'd all been for the previous two nights. Some members of their group had rented a VIP suite and, while they were on one side, the family and the others stood on the opposite side so they could all talk.

Ginger focused on Jake as his cellphone chortled. She shook her head because she knew what was coming next.

Chapter 2
Jake

"Dad, you guys should come over here. Jake Owen,
was so awesome."

"Who's on now?"

"Maren Morris... Listen."

Connor's speech had a slight slur to it, and the music
intensified as Jake assumed he held up his phone. He
chuckled with a teasing air as the cab stopped at the light.

"Come on!" a chorus of similar requests chirped out
of the speaker.

For some incomprehensible reason, their kids
adored their parents. So did all their friends, and even
though it was unusual for college age kids, it flattered the
couple nonetheless. He glanced over at Ginger, her red
hair flaming in the sun, and pulled the cellphone away
from his face.

"They require our presence."

"No." She snickered as he raised his eyebrows in
challenge. "They require *your* presence. I'm going to
tackle that room."

Jake grinned and gave his wife a kiss before handing
her the beach bag.

"Okay, I'm coming," he said to Connor, then to the
driver called out, "I'll get out here."

As Jake crossed through the stopped cars and
stepped onto the sidewalk, he reached into his back
pocket for his wallet and found it empty. Patting his front

pockets, he found them empty too. Jake glanced up quickly, as the cab containing his wife moved through the intersection.

"Well, shit," he chuckled, and started to jog. He made it to the hotel portico just as Ginger walked through the automatic sliders.

"Ging," he hailed, and she turned, looking puzzled. "You got my money. It's in the bag."

"Oh, no," she said, and pawed through the contents to retrieve his wallet, then held it out to him. "Here ya go."

Studying the wallet, then the crowded street, and past it to the crowded assembly behind the fence, he frowned. A hot mass of humanity, pooled in the center that they called the pit. He glanced back at his wife. The doors of the hotel and casino sprang open, emitting the cool breeze of the air conditioner.

"Screw it, I'm gonna play some blackjack."

Ginger shook her head and walked through the doors with him. Once inside they separated with another kiss, Jake to the casino floor, and Ginger toward the elevators.

Chapter 3
Connor

The day was one of his best. Connor was never so content as with a beer in his hand, dancing with an extensive group of people at a country music concert. Every one of his favorite artists performed, and before him now was the concert's headliner, Jason Aldean, crooning about taking a ride on a green tractor.

At six-foot-five, Connor stood several inches taller than most of the surrounding people, but he blended in with them just the same. Alcohol buzzed around his head as he danced with everyone in the pit. Closing his brilliant blue eyes, he just felt bliss. When he opened them again, he glimpsed his sister gesticulating at her cellphone. He withdrew his own phone from his pocket and saw she'd left a text.

—*Dad isn't coming after all. You got the card. Come out and I'll get you more beer.*—

Grinning, Connor held up his cup in a salute that he was coming. Dancing his way out of the center throng to his sister, he handed her the credit card they shared for the night.

"Nice," he teased, nodding up at the thick floral wreath she had dragged him over to buy an hour earlier.

Now, it lay askew on her soft caramel hair. He snorted and tried to straighten it at the same time Faith did, causing it to once again shift cockeyed.

"What do you want?" she yelled, leaning close to his

ear.

"Um, Bud Lime."

"Okay. Don't go back in there yet because you won't hear me when I come back."

Connor nodded his head in understanding, then saw his friend, Josh, dancing with his girlfriend, Nia. Connor's own girlfriend, Naomi, couldn't make the weekend run, and for a moment he missed her presence. As his sister started to walk away, Nia called after her.

"Wait, Faith. I'll go with you."

The boys looked at each other with simultaneous grins and raised their beers.

Chapter 4
Faith

The young women walked to the beer stand, and Faith blew out a sigh at the lengthy line awaiting them. She plucked out her cellphone from her bra and texted her mom, typing with a smirk.

—Connor's messed up!—

She felt quite tipsy herself, she observed, and slipped the phone back into place before turning to Nia.

"What are you getting?"

"Just a beer for Josh. I have to get up early for work tomorrow," Nia said with regret.

"Adulting sucks," Faith remarked.

"Doesn't it?" Nia replied with a laugh.

The girls watched everyone around them feeling the music with stupid grins on their faces and singing the words as loud as they could. Nia chuckled and checked her own cellphone.

Once she arrived at the front of the line, Faith requested three beers, and a bottled water for Nia. Upon receiving the beverages, the girls walked back to their group. As they approached, Faith noticed her gregarious brother edging back into the periphery of the pit and reached out a quelling hand.

"My sister," he sang, seeing her and taking two of the proffered beverages.

As Connor turned to go back into the throng of dancers, Josh reached out a hand and snagged one beer.

Their large group collected on the outside rail of the second VIP suite, and began to sing, *When She Says Baby*, captivating her brother's attention once more. He circled back and sang with them. Faith felt her phone vibrate and saw her mom had texted back on their family group chat.

—How messed up?—

She was about to reply when she realized someone was lighting off some firecrackers. She turned her head and watched the dirt floor plume up next to her as if by its own accord and thought, *that's weird.*

Chapter 5
Ginger

Ginger walked into their room on the twenty-seventh floor, and it was as she feared. Discarded clothing, makeup, and hair products with the caps off, spread across every inch of the floor's surface. *That's what happens when four kids prepare to get ready for an event in a small room.*

Sighing, she walked to the bathroom, used it, then washed her hands and the sunscreen from her face. She squinted at her reflection. *Not old yet, but not young anymore either.* Shrugging, she turned back to get started on the room when her phone pinged with a text from her daughter.

—Connor's messed up!—

Ginger shook her head a little, then frowned. Was Faith just telling her or did her son need some help? She tried to call her daughter's cell but the command to leave a message sounded.

"How messed up?" she asked, then ended the call. Thinking better of it, she also texted it out, in case Faith couldn't hear the voice message above the music.

Receiving no response, the mother just raised her eyebrows, pursed her lips, and started sorting clothing piles on the floor. Her cellphone buzzed, and noted the caller was Connor. *Odd.* Her son wasn't the best about calling in mundane times and never when a fun event was in full swing. She accepted the call.

"Hey Con, I hear you're…" A strange noise popped out from the line. "Con?"

The call disconnected. Baffled, Ginger looked at her daughter's message again. A dark and cold foreboding permeated her, seeping into her bones. Her hands shook as she punched in characters.

—I want to know what's going on with my son, NOW!—

She hit send, and a few seconds later the phone rang. Again, it was from Connor, not Faith.

"Connor?" Ginger barked out in a panic. "Connor?" The strange popping noises were there again and like the first call, the line cut off. "What in the hell?" She heard the firecracker noises for a third time, only now, they were outside her window. "What *is* that?"

Ginger looked back down at her phone as her eyes began to sting. She stabbed in the digits for her husband's cell.

"Jake," she said, as soon as he answered. "Something's very wrong…"

"Ginger," he said, talking over her. "Someone's shooting."

"What?"

"They said there's an active shooting going on in the hotel. Stay in the room."

Her world tunneled, and she ran to the window where swarms of ant-like people were running from the heart of the pit.

"Are you…" Just then her phone beeped and Faith's picture lit up her screen. "It's Faith."

"Call me back."

"Okay," she said and switched callers. "Faith?" The inhuman noise that came from her daughter stabbed through Ginger's heart. Her stomach fell like someone had opened the floor below her. "Faith!" she yelled. "Talk to me! Faith!"

"Mama. They're shooting! Someone's shooting. There's people…people are dying… Oh, God!"

"Faith, where are you? Are you with Connor?"

"Yes."

"Are you both okay?"

"Yes! Mama, they're shooting people."

"Where are you?"

"I-I don't know… In the VIP thing!"

"Okay." Ginger raced to the window and peered down again. The throngs of people were still moving outward in every direction. "Are you where we were last night?"

"Mom."

"Faith?" She heard her daughter cry out and again the phone went dead.

"Oh my God." Ginger raised a hand to her mouth and moaned, before whispering, "Please, Holy Father, don't take my children."

Chapter 6
Connor and Faith

Connor noticed Faith glance down at the dirt, then back up in confusion. There were other people around them doing the same thing. The firecrackers went off again, but somehow they didn't sound right.

"Connor," his sister said, face draining of color. "I think someone's shooting a gun."

Connor knew his way around guns and shook his head, trying to convince them both.

"No. There's no way anyone could get inside here with a gun. We went through metal detectors." He looked around and saw people running. Some tripped and fell, as he heard Nia call out to Josh to run.

The couple joined hands and sprinted down the fence line. Time moved in slow motion. Connor's arms and legs felt sluggish as if trapped in mud. The shooting came from across the pit and sounded like an automatic machine gun.

In the blink of an eye the concert goers stampeded in a panic and shoved his sister into him. They fell hard, and his breath expelled from his lungs. Terrified they had hurt her, Connor looked into her frightened green eyes, and she blinked back at him.

"Are you okay?"

"Yeah," she said, voice quivering. "We have to get out of here. Now."

Instantly, the happy buzz of earlier steamed off his

brain. Connor looked up and saw hundreds of people purging themselves from the pit toward the chain-link fences, desperate for escape. Others fell, clutching their bodies and screaming out in pain. His eyes darted around. It seemed to him that the shooting shifted and was coming from somewhere different now. *Multiple shooters, inside the arena? How the hell did they get in?* The people in the middle were the targets. Blanching, he recognized he'd just been in the middle. As bullets sprayed back and forth, he, like his sister, realized they needed to move away from the belly of the beast.

****

Faith stood quickly, jerking Conner to his feet. She continued to hold his hand as she half pulled and half dragged him to the stoop of the VIP suite and pounded on the closed door.

"Open the door!" she screamed.

Faith looked to her right where a wall of people stood at the fence line. Some were crawling over it, some trying to force it down. A few people collapsed to the ground, not moving. Others had people laying over them in protection. Frantic, she turned and pounded on the door along with her brother.

"Please!" she screamed. "Please, don't let us die out here!"

The door opened, and Connor shoved her inside before following. Six or seven people huddled in the modest room. Faith withdrew her phone and stabbed in some digits. She took her first real breath, and upon hearing her mother's familiar voice, howled into the phone. Faith answered Ginger's questions, but when she glanced up and her vision sharpened on the front wall of the shack, she stopped. Light streamed in from tiny holes

278

all over the siding. *Holes... Bullet holes.* She heard them ping off the metal railings on the seating above. Faith, lowered the phone, disconnecting the call with her mother on accident. Her mind blanked, and she froze in fear as Connor turned to her.

"We can't stay here, Faith."

The pinging moved down the shack but returned just as fast. She heard people screaming outside, and the souls above them trying to get down.

"No, we're safer in here. We're safe."

He brought his face to within inches of hers. "No, we aren't. We're just sitting here. It's like we're out there. These walls won't stop shit. Now look," he said, eyes gesturing behind her.

Faith followed his gaze. The back door of the shack shifted ajar. She could see people pushing down the fence.

"Come on."

Without another word, Connor grabbed her hand and yanked her out the door. Several people ran around behind the stage now, and into the street. The whistling of the bullets and thuds into the earth had moved off into the distance, to the other side of the pit. Her brother looked back at her and grasped her hand tighter.

"We got this." Connor gave a quick scan of the scene one last time, then yelled, "Run!"

She had time to nod once before they darted for cover behind the stage. A flood of people, cars, and trucks now streamed into the street. Josh and Nia appeared in her line of sight, jumping into the back of a white pickup truck, the girl's tiny frame disappearing under stacks of people. The tires screeched, and the truck drove away. Relief they were alive spurted through

Faith. All around them chaos reigned, as once inebriated people were now behind the wheels of their automobiles. Connor jerked her hand to move with him.

"We're gonna get killed by a car if we don't get out of here," he screamed.

They ran down the street toward Mandalay Bay, but a police officer directed them a different way. At his feet lay a girl, surrounded by a pool of blood. Connor looked around and gestured at a quieter side street. They reached some parked cars and hid between the front and back bumpers of two.

Faith's hand in his began to shake violently as she realized what she'd witnessed. People weren't tripping because they stumbled. The girl down the street wasn't just injured. Her confidence in escape began to waver.

"C-Connor, I can't do this," she said, eyes wild. "I… that girl…"

"Yes, we can, Faith." He placed gentle hands to the sides of her face. "Look at me. Faith look at me." He gave her a little shake, and she did. "We're okay, ya know. We're alive. You're okay… I'm okay. We are both going to be fine." He stared into her eyes as she came back to her senses. "All right?" he asked, and she nodded. "Okay. We're going to the hotel, then we'll get up to the room to Mom and Dad."

"Yeah," she said, nodding her head, with more assurance. "Okay."

He released her face and once more placed her hand in his.

Chapter 7
Jake

Jake received his cards and watched as the dealer dealt the hand out to the others. His cellphone rang, revealing his son's number, and he picked it up.

"Con, hold on," he said, setting the phone down and playing his hand of blackjack. A twenty revealed itself and he smiled, then picked up the phone again, "Hey, you're never gonna guess what just happened."

He waited for his son to respond but heard nothing. Looking down, he discovered the call disconnected. *Butt dial?* He shrugged and looked up as a crowd of people began running down the hallway and out of the casino area. *People don't run in casinos.*

Jake looked back at the dealer, and asked, "What's going on?"

The dealer watched the crowd too, then directed his gaze to his pit boss. Looking confused, the pit boss, strode to the phone and dialed some numbers. Gamblers sitting at tables around Jake started picking up their chips and money, then melted in with the crowd. The pit boss hung up and announced, "There is an active shooting going on." At this declaration, even more people left, so Jake picked up his belongings too. He stood and approached the large moving mass. Trying to understand what was happening, he remembered Connor's strange call. He pulled out his phone and tried to call his son back, but it went to voicemail. He tried again with the same result.

Oh, fuck. The father's heart began to race, when his phone buzzed in his hand. Seeing the picture he took of his wife right after she woke up one morning, he connected the call.

"Jake," she said, as soon as he answered. "Something very wrong…"

"Ginger," he said, talking over her. "Someone's shooting."

"What?"

"They said there's an active shooting going on in the hotel. Stay in the room."

"Are you…" she paused, then said, "It's Faith."

"Call me back."

"Okay."

Jake ran outside and somehow knew he shouldn't be there. Running back inside, he moved along with the humanity into the food atrium, near an aquarium sign. Looking down at his phone, he pushed the button to check the time, and willed it to ring, but the screen remained black. Realizing he'd been on it all day, playing music, doing some work, and taking pictures, he pushed the button again, with no result, and now understood his communication was cut off. Picturing the faces of the most important people in his life, Jake looked around the mass congregation and noticed a pole with a house phone on it. He crossed over to it before anyone else could, picked up the receiver, and dialed their room number.

"Hello?"

"Ginger?"

"Faith called and said they were in the VIP shack. I think where we were standing last night by the

Andersons." Ginger paused. "S-she said people were dying. Oh, God, Jake! How does she know that?" Panicked, he tried to think, as she asked, "Where are you?"

"I left the floor. I'm over by the deli where we ate lunch at yesterday, but my phone's dead. This is a house phone."

"Did they say what's happening?"

"They just said someone was shooting, but I don't think they know who or where or how many."

"Well, someone's shooting in the crowd over there." They were silent, only listening to each other breathe for several seconds. "They went into the shack thing," Ginger said again, breaking the silence.

"But they're okay?"

"I think so. She…" there was a pause, "Oh, God, okay, that's her."

"Find out where they are but stay on the line with me and put yours on speaker."

"Okay," Ginger did as instructed, then said to their daughter, "Faith?"

"Mom."

Jake heard his daughter's frightened voice and felt complete helplessness for the first time in his life.

"Okay, baby," her mother soothed. "It's okay. I love you guys so much. So much. Where are you now?"

"I-I don't know. There's blood… A lot of blood in the street."

"Okay, honey. We will get you guys out of there. Can you find out where you are? Are you or Connor hurt?"

"He's here…he's…we aren't hurt. We're at the hotel."

"At Mandalay?" Ginger's voice sounded shocked.

"Yes."

"No!" Ginger screamed.

"Tell them the shooter's here," Jake said, heart skipping a beat too.

"Faith, stop. Stop!" Ginger yelled. "The shooter's here. Do not come in here!"

"But we're already here."

Connor's voice boomed down the line, "We're downstairs behind the concierge thingy."

"You need to leave!"

"Where are we supposed to go?" Everyone went silent because no one knew the answer. "We're going to try to make our way up to you."

"No," Ginger commanded. "Go find someplace to hide right now. Then call or text me when you're hidden. Okay?"

"Okay."

"I love you. We love you both so much."

"I love you too."

Chapter 8
Connor and Faith

Connor looked around the concierge podium they hid behind, and Faith followed suit. The immense casino floor was empty. All they could hear was pings and electronic melodies from hundreds of slot machines. The rest was an eerie ghost town.

An open-air bar near the entrance beckoned. He looked at his sister and pointed to it, and she nodded. First she turned to remove her heeled boots, so she could run faster in her bare feet. Crossing the distance, they ducked under the walkthrough and behind the bar, crouching low on the floor. There was no movement, no sound. As the adrenaline waned a bit, both started to shake again. Connor, worried they'd make unwelcome noise, noticed a bottle of Vodka sitting on the counter. He grabbed it and a soda nozzle from the counter, and swallowed a shot, feeling the heat slide down his throat, before chasing it with some Sprite.

"Who-wa," he whispered, making a face, and gestured for Faith to open her mouth.

He repeated the actions with her, then they settled down to wait. Faith took out her phone and pushed the top button.

"My battery's dead," she whispered. "How about you?"

Connor looked at his phone, and whispered back, "Like sixteen percent."

Faith pulled up their mother's number on his phone and hit enter, before handing it to her brother.

"Connor?" she asked. "Where are you, baby?"

"We're in an open bar thing."

"Okay." She sounded relieved.

"Can we come up there?"

"No, I tried to go out and there's a SWAT guy next to the elevators and stairs," his mother replied. "He said no one leaves. No one comes up." She paused for a minute, as if listening to something. "Dad's on the house phone. He wants to know exactly where you're at."

Connor looked around, then at Faith. "Where are we?"

She glanced around too and saw a coaster. "The Orchid Lounge."

"Orchid Lounge, Mom."

She paused again, and he heard the faint words of his father.

"Okay, Connor? Dad said to stay right there. Do not move. They're sending the SWAT people in there to get you guys."

"Okay," Connor acknowledged, then closed his eyes and leaned his head back against the wall.

Chapter 9
Jake

Jake listened to his wife's instructions to their children to find shelter. He tried to hear more, but a man wearing a shirt with the hotel logo approached him with an officer in tactical gear.

"Excuse me, sir," the staffer said. "You need to hang that up."

"No," Jake responded.

"No?" the man parroted, as if he hadn't heard him correctly. "Sir, we need this…"

"My kids have been running for their life, and they are hiding out front somewhere. You've trapped my wife upstairs, I've run out of battery, and there's someone out there shooting innocent people, and you don't know who or where they are," Jake spat with venom. "I'm not giving you this fucking phone."

The hotel man stared at him with irritation, while the officer asked, "Where exactly are your kids?"

"Ginger?" he spoke into the phone. "The police are here and they want to know exactly where the kids are so they can go get them." He listened, then covered the mouthpiece. "They're hiding behind a bar called the Orchid Lounge, near a concierge desk."

"Okay," the officer said. "We'll go get them." Flooding with relief, Jake listened to the instructions from the officer.

"Ginger?" Jake said, looking at the staffer that stared

back at him with a pinched face. He showed the man his back. "The kids need to respond when they call out to them and put their hands up first when they stand up. Okay?"

"Okay," she said. "Faith's phone is dead and Connor's almost out of battery too. We have to hang up for a while."

"Agreed. Tell them to conserve it. They're making me give up this phone too, but I'll get a hold of you somehow. Just try to get the kids in one place, and I'll get to them."

"Okay. The neighbor here told me they think the shooter's moved to another hotel."

"Jesus." Jake gave a sharp exhale. "We're hearing rumors they may have shot one already."

"Are you safe where you're at?" she asked.

"There's a shit-ton of cops, and like SWAT everywhere."

"Okay." She exhaled. "I love you."

"Love you too, babe." He severed the call but felt like he was severing a limb in doing so.

Chapter 10
Ginger

A short time later, Faith told her mother, the police came, searched them, then gave them instructions to go to a random exit, without an escort. However, when they arrived in the area, no one was there to direct them. Standing in front of the House of Blues, a short distance away, and feeling vulnerable, Faith and Connor took refuge inside under a table by the kitchen to wait.

The hardest thing Ginger ever did was disconnect from her family then. The room grew silent as she paced, then stared out the window at the police and rescue vehicles dotted along the street. She packed and repacked their bags until the room was spotless. Horrible images came to her in abysmal color—her children hiding, and evil gunmen rushing in to find them and shoot them on a dirty restaurant floor. Their last vision on earth, crazy dead eyes of madmen staring back at them. She shook her head in an effort to clear the vision.

A knock sounded at her door, and for a moment her heart skipped a beat as she opened it.

"Hands up!" screamed several men in full military gear, as the surrounding doors opened. "Get your hands up! Get them up! Where I can see them!"

Ginger expelled a hard breath and raised her hands. A semi-automatic rifle hovered four inches off her center mass. She was stunned into silence as they motioned her into the hall.

The hotel floors were laid out in a quad formation—two doors close together, two doors on the opposite side of the hall, a section of the hallway, then the next quad of doors. As four men from a tactical team held the occupants of the rooms at gunpoint in the hall, sixteen men, four for each room, searched the individual areas.

"Can we leave after this?" one occupant asked.

"No," was all one man said.

"My kids were at the concert and are downstairs hiding. Can they come up here? Please. They're scared," Ginger asked.

"No," the man said again.

"Are we in danger here?" an occupant of another room asked, but the man ignored them.

When all was clear, the men left as quick as they'd come, continuing down the hall. Ginger walked back into her room and stared at the white walls. On legs no longer able to support her, she gave in and crumpled to the floor. Once there, she folded her hands and prayed as she sobbed. Feelings of guilt at the inability to protect her kids overwhelmed her. Tears streamed down her face as the first promises she ever made to her children shattered. There were monsters in the world after all.

Chapter 11
Connor and Faith

After a couple hours, officers liberated the siblings from their hiding place. They moved through the hotel toward the parking garage. As they progressed, more people came out of hiding. They were searched before they could join the group, as the collective lay on their stomachs, hands locked behind their heads, at gunpoint, until they were told they could stand again. Upon entering the garage, the Hughes kids were taken to an area with hundreds of other individuals, all milling about, and told to wait. Connor paced as more and more people congregated. As the crowd grew, so did his obvious anxiety. Her brother's phone buzzed in her pocket, and Faith withdrew it, connecting the call.

"Mom?"

"Hi, honey," her voiced soothed like a salve on Faith's jittery nerves. "Where did they take you?"

"It's just outside a parking garage."

"Here at the hotel?"

"Yeah."

"How long do you have to stay there?"

"Tell her I want to go," Connor proclaimed. "I want to get out of here."

"Mom, Connor wants to leave, but earlier they said we couldn't."

"I think it's because they don't know where all the shooters are. We heard they could be at other hotels now."

"I don't like this at all," Connor said, grabbing the phone. "We aren't safe here. I want to get the fuck out of here, Mom," he said again.

"Can you leave?" his mother asked. "Is there a way to?"

Faith, also listening at the phone, looked around. There were police in the garage, but people also wandered around. She took the phone from her brother.

"I think so. They told us to stay here at first but people are walking all over the place, and they don't seem to care."

"Okay, well, Dad doesn't have a phone, but he said for us to pick a place for him to meet you. He'll call me as soon as he can." She paused. "I want it away from the hotel though. Do you think you could find the big Welcome to Las Vegas sign?"

Faith looked over at her brother, and they nodded at each other.

"Yeah," they said in unison.

"Okay, how much battery do you have left?" she asked.

"Four percent," Faith responded.

"That's it?"

"Yeah."

"Okay, do not waste any of it. Just my calls, okay?"

"Okay."

"All right. If you can get away safely, start heading to the sign, and just text me, don't call. I love you."

"Okay. I love you too."

After they disconnected, the kids moved to the outer region of the group, then disappeared down the street.

Chapter 12
Ginger

They were so close. If they could just find each other, everything would be okay. In Ginger's mind, that was all that mattered. They just needed to find each other. Her cellphone rang.

"Hello?" she asked the unfamiliar number.

"It's me," her husband replied. "An EMT let me use her phone for a second."

"Okay, well, the kids just texted. They're going to the Welcome to Las Vegas sign."

"That's a mile and a half away."

"Well, I wanted them away from the hotel," Ginger retorted with irritation. "It was the easiest thing to think of."

"No," he said. "You're right…sorry. They released us so I'll head over. Just tell them to wait there if they get there before I do, and not go anywhere else."

"Okay. They're almost out of the battery, so call *me* if you need to."

"Okay."

Now all she could do was wait. She tried to call down to the front desk again, but the phone just rang and rang. Anger seared through her at the absence of information from anyone over the past six hours. The police, the resort, neither said a word to the people in the hotel towers about what transpired, what was happening, or when they could leave.

She wouldn't be right or centered until she could wrap her arms around her children and know in her soul they were safe.

The room was too quiet. Glancing up she studied the television. She never even thought to turn it on. Sitting on the bed, she clicked the power button, and the gray light solidified into a colored picture. A reporter was a few feet away from the Las Vegas sign, and they pointed the camera toward Mandalay Bay. Ginger sprang off the bed scanning the background behind the reporter, searching for a glimpse of someone she loved. The woman's words solidified as the picture morphed into a tall blond man, in a gray Hawks jersey and ugly orange swim trunks, his arms opened wide.

Ginger stared at the picture in disbelief, watching her children throw themselves into their father's arms. The three made a tight, united circle, clinging to one another in relief. Ginger walked to the screen and touched each of their images.

"There you are," she said in heaving sobs. "There you are."

As the reporter approached them, Connor looked over. His eyes were wider than she'd ever seen them, and they didn't seem to blink. Shock and trauma radiated from his eyes, and for a moment she didn't recognize him. Looking to Faith, the same expression lingered there, and she wondered how much they'd witnessed and endured to warrant it.

Jake walked over, bringing arms around them both, and drew them in close to him. His gaze drifted to the camera, and into his wife's eyes. She knew he was telling her he had them, and that they were safe.

****

Several hours later, Ginger heard a commotion in the hallway. She opened the door and realized new guests were going into their rooms.

"Hey," she called out, and the couple looked up. "Did you just check in?"

"Yeah," the man replied with a genuine laugh. "You should see it down there. It's a zoo."

The light-hearted tone, implying the night before hadn't happened and that today was like any other, angered her. The hotel was open, and no one said a word.

A bus transported Jake and the kids to UNLV and from there a taxi drove them to the airport. The adrenaline, used in its entirety, caused Faith to vomit, then fall asleep with Connor's head in her lap. Their parents tried to decide the best course of action. They could possibly miss their flight and wait until Ginger could leave the hotel, or they could take their flights, and she would drive the five hours to Cheney and see them the next day.

"Just get them the hell out of here," she said, knowing what it cost her.

She had six suitcases and four carry-on bags to transport from the hotel to the airport. Anything not belonging to her family, she brought with her, knowing the kids would make sure their rightful owners retrieved them.

Infuriated, not wanting to wait a second longer than necessary, she walked to the lobby and to the long line in front of the check-in counter, where a haggard-looking woman made proclamations.

"We will check people out in a systematic order. We'll call you when…"

Ignoring the woman, like they ignored their guests,

Ginger looked around. A bellman stood nearby trying to sort through the bags. She approached him, with the only smile she could muster.

"Sir, I have two children that were there last night. I have their luggage and my luggage and my husband's…"

"Ma'am, I'm sorry, I can't…"

"No, no, no," she blurted, and raised her hands. "Please, I just need one of these roller things. I'll do everything else myself."

Relief and sympathy spread across his kind face, and he walked over to retrieve a luggage cart and rolled it back over to her.

"Go down to the garage level. They have shuttles set up to go to the airport. Just go in that line. Don't take no for an answer." He gave her a conspiratorial wink before bending back to his task.

Ginger loaded the bags and found herself in the same spot her children had occupied, just a few hours prior. Most people waiting had a lot of people with few bags, so the smaller cabs weren't as helpful. However, Ginger was one person with many bags and received a taxi rather quickly.

As she settled into the cab, and they turned the corner, she saw the carnage of the night before for the first time. Backpacks, shoes, hats, clothing, cups, glasses, cellphones, chairs, and a vast array of other items spread out over the now abandoned lot. As the arena vanished from her eye line, she leaned back in her seat and closed her eyes for the first time in twenty-seven hours. Tears slid down her face as she thought of the hundreds of people now killed or injured. And the deep psychological damage to come, that would not be easy to tame. Families whose homecomings wouldn't be so happy but devastating and life altering. Her heart shattered for them.

Her cellphone buzzed with a text, and she glanced down at it. Illuminated on the screen was a picture of her family, holding up a small ragged piece of paper.

We're waiting for you!

Ginger continued to cry, and though she could see her driver checking on her in the mirror, he thankfully said nothing. Arriving at the airport, they pulled up to the curb, and she got out, searching but not seeing them.

"Mama," Faith said, and Ginger turned around to see tears streaming down her daughter's face.

Connor stood next to her, hollowed eyed, and Jake behind him. Ginger let out a sob and held out her arms, as her family raced to embrace her. She looked up into the bright blue of the October sky, with the sun its only occupant once more, and realized every October first from then on they'd be dancing, maybe through tears, but they'd be dancing… together.

Thank you for purchasing
this publication of The Wild Rose Press, Inc.

For questions or more information
contact us at
info@thewildrosepress.com.

The Wild Rose Press, Inc.
www.thewildrosepress.com